IN THE TALL

PINES

BY
ANDREW HOPKINS

FIDDLEHEAD PUBLISHING
CLAREMONT NH 03743

ISBN 978-0-692-91258-4

Printer: Lulu publishing

Printed in the United States of America

Fiddlehead Publishing
12 Manville Ave.
Claremont NH 03743

Photography by Andrew Hopkins
Front cover photo taken at the Bradford Pines, Bradford NH
Back cover photo taken by permission at The Fort at Number Four, Charlestown NH

About the author:

Andy Hopkins is a lifelong New Hampshire resident with a burning curiosity about the regions forgotten past. He started writing IN THE TALL PINES while earning his BA in American Studies from Granite State College in 2009. IN THE TALL PINES is the exciting culmination of years of work and study on the early history of New England.

To: My Grandfather Clyde E. Papps who was a fisherman, an inventor, a worker at Dartmouth Woolen in Claremont NH, a lifelong New Hampshire resident, and an inspiration for my life.

Intentionally left blank.

Chapter 1

"Timber!" A cry of warning rings out from the primeval forest on the banks of the Connecticut River as a towering two hundred year old Eastern White Pine tree finally begins to yield to the eighteenth century New Hampshire colonist's incessant chopping and sawing at its trunk. The majestic twenty-story tall spire starts to sway, and with a loud crack suddenly gives in to its battle with natural forces, tumbling onto the mat of the ancient woodland floor with an enormous surrendering crash.

Alarmed by the unexpected clatter, forest birds and animals scatter in every direction while their screams of warning pierce and echo down the formerly serene calm of the river valley. Nether lying plants squint as rays of afternoon sunlight now pierce through a new clearing in the forest where the shadow of the giant had reigned for centuries before.

Through the clouds of settling debris, a jubilant Nathaniel Jarvis clambers to the top of the massive tree trunk smiling and victoriously raises his ax claiming his prize. He shouts down to his son Benjamin as he excitedly surveys the fallen Goliath lying at his feet, "This one's a beauty, Ben! She'll fetch a tidy sum at the sawmill down at Number Four, or even more if we float her down river to the Massachusetts mills with the spring log drive."

He begins to do a dance on the tree trunk feigning royalty, and shouts out, "I imagine the almighty King of England, if he had his way about it, would like her better as a mast for one of his warships, but the way I see it, His Majesty George the Third already has his riches, and now we can begin to lay claim to our own… This land is filled with these beauties my boy, prime for our axes." Continuing to clown, he pauses to make an exaggerated royal bow and adds, "I can see more than enough of these giant white pines here on our land grant to make us the new Dukes of the Colony of New Hampshire."

He jumps down off of the tree trunk smiling and eagerly shakes his son's hand saying, "We did it Ben, another bounty from our land. If this hilly land full of rocks holds nothing else for us, at least we'll be able to make a go of it here by cutting down the pines. She is a beauty."

"She sure is a beauty father! I believe no one in England has ever set eyes on as bonny a 200 foot specimen such as this one!" says Benjamin excitedly as he too starts to do a royal dance, mimicking his father. Nathaniel Jarvis chuckles and adds, "Aye, Ben, I bet the lot of them have never seen a tree over 20 foot tall, 'cept in a printed picture book. They can't even imagine a land such as this where trees have grown untouched for more years than we can ever count. Now let's get limbing her before the sun sets on us again."

"Yes sir!" Ben nods in agreement as he begins hacking away at the furry pine bows, quickly adding, "I'm tasting Mum's mutton stew as we speak, and the growl in my stomach's saying don't keep her waiting." Nathaniel smiles and replies, "Keep your mind on your ax, and your belly will wait." Ben recants obediently with a nod, "Yes father, work and chores first, lest the devil creep into idle hands." Nathaniel answers proudly, "That's my boy!" As the midsummer sun begins to dip into the crimson western New England sky.

It's the summer of 1765 and Benning Wentworth, the Royal Governor of the Colony of New Hampshire, has been making land grants in the unsettled areas between the Maine, Massachusetts, and New York borders. The New England colonies were poor after fighting the French and Indian War, and the grants were made because they were the only way the colonies had to pay their debts from the war.

Nathaniel Jarvis received his grant for his service in the war and is attempting to clear the age-old forest to build a homestead for his young family in the present day City of Claremont New Hampshire on the eastern banks of the Connecticut River. This area of New England had been unsettleable prior to this time by the English, as the Native American tribe known as the Abenaki had controlled it. These lands were pristine old-growth forests that had been inhabited only by the Native American tribes for several thousand years.

He looks over at Ben and pauses to reflect. Thinking back to his own father's farm years before, Nathaniel remembers how he was like Ben at his age, tired of the endless chopping and clearing, and a growing boy tends to worry more about his next dinner than work. He pauses and wonders if he's made the right decision by leaving their family and friends safe at home in colonial Massachusetts and bringing his new family north into the wilderness of New Hampshire.

The forests in Massachusetts had been mostly cleared of the giant pine trees by the time Ben was born, and work for a woodsman was becoming harder and harder to find. Nathaniel had come north to New Hampshire hoping for a better life for his family, but life in the wilderness was more difficult than he expected. The forests were bountiful, but with only two working the land, it took much longer to cut down the trees and with the sawmills being several miles down river, it also took more time to bring the cut trees to the mill to be sawn into boards here than it did in Massachusetts where at the time there were sawmills on most every stream. Feeling a bit sobered; Nathaniel looks up to the heavens for guidance, as Ben starts piling the limbs of the giant tree up on the ground.

"What are you doing Father?" Ben yells, as he sees his father pause, "Time's a wastin, and these branches won't chop themselves off!" His father smilingly replies, "Who taught you that? I'd cleared 40 or 50 acres by the time I was your age. You've got some catching up to do before you can talk to me! Keep your mind on your axe and we'll be home for Mum's supper in no time." Ben grins as he continues to swing his axe, knowing he's struck a chord with his father. As twilight starts to fill the sky, they wipe the sweat from their brows, and call it a day.

Walking back down the forest path to their homestead Ben asks, "Didn't I see the King's Broad Arrow mark on that big pine we cut today, Father? Mother told me that we weren't supposed to cut any trees that had that Broad Arrow Mark on them or we would get in a lot of trouble with the Governor." His father answers, "My axe took care of that burden, they'll notice no Kings Broad Arrow Mark on that one. This land is covered with these mighty pines, and we must realize that God, and not the King, owns the trees and the sky. The King can sit in his ivory tower and rule the Empire, but we colonists are scraping for our own survival in the untamed wilderness of the New World."

"The giant pines are the most valuable things on our land. We have many other types of trees here, but none have wood as suitable for building with as these giant white pines. The wood is light, strong and these trees have grown straighter, taller, and wider than the other trees so it's easier to get longer, truer boards out of the old pines than any other tree on our property. We would have had much more difficulty trying to build our cabin with an Oak or an Elm tree whose wood is much harder to cut, not as straight, and are usually full of knots from all of the branches."

"You know how hard it is to cut into a board with knots in it don't you son? Remember the cedar chest we were making a few weeks ago?" Ben answers, "I sure do. I sawed and sawed on those boards, and it took me *forever* just to cut one board to size." His father answers smiling, "Well it wasn't *forever* my boy, but it did take considerably longer to make that chest with cedar. Your Mother wanted a cedar chest though, and I can't blame her, cedar does make the best chests for storing clothes and things. Aren't you glad we didn't have to make the whole cabin out of cedar?" Ben quickly nods in agreement, and asks, "But what does the

King's Broad Arrow Mark really mean father? These trees are on our land grant. Why can't we cut them down?"

Nathaniel sits Ben down on the stump of the newly cut tree and looking Ben in the eye says, "Well Ben, the King's Broad Arrow Mark means two things son: First it means that the King is an ocean away but he still wants to keep the colonists under his thumb as if we were still in England. Second is that the almighty King will punish us if he catches us cutting down the marked trees. You see, he wants to take our biggest pine trees to use as masts to build the fastest ships in the world for the British navy, so England can rule the whole known world, even though we New England colonists need them to build houses and buildings to survive the cold winters here. The strong light pine wood makes the giant white pine trees a great prize back in England."

Nathaniel continues, "We colonists were selling these trees ourselves, and making a go of it here back when we started the colonies. The King saw all of the profit we were making and decided to keep the trees for his own profit and use. He sent thousands of red-coated "Surveyors of the King's Woods" out across this land to mark all of the large pines. They marked trees from Connecticut to Maine forbidding them to be cut down except for the King's own uses."

"His laws on the size of white pines we were allowed to cut for our own use started at less than twenty-four inches in diameter, but he's been continually lowering that size over the years and there's word now that he will drop it to twelve inches or less for colonist's use soon."

"He granted us these colonies here in America, gave us each titles to the land, and then told us we couldn't cut the trees for our own use. As this land is covered with these trees and many more natural resources, but nothing of more value, how are we colonists supposed to make a go of it here when we can't use the most valuable ware on the property to raise the funds we desperately need to civilize this wilderness? There are many of us here who feel this way, and talk is turning more and more in the colonies to a separation from England and the king's ridiculous demands."

Ben replies, "Thank you for the explanation, father, and I don't see why a rich king needs to take our pine trees either. He has the whole world, at least he could spare us our trees." Nathaniel replies, " I wish he would, son, for all of our sakes, I wish he would."

He pauses and adds, "Now let's get on home. Your Mother's supper is waiting, and we don't want to allow Rebecca's fine cooking to spoil." They get up from the stump and wearily make their way down the forest trail to their homestead.

Rebecca smiles seeing her husband and son drag into the cabin. "Another rough day boys?" She asks, holding their newly born daughter Katherine in one arm and a bucket of freshly picked elderberries in the other. "Just like any of them," answers Nathaniel taking a handful of elderberries and giving her a kiss. "Cleared land's civilized, and the wilds of the woods belong to the devil. We don't want the devil disturbing you and little baby Katherine now do we?" The baby smiles recognizing her father's voice as she happily chews on a piece of soggy toast. "There's my happy girl, it does my heart wonders just to see you smile. Makes a hard day's work in the wilds almost seem worth it."

"Worth it, I hope so," his wife replies, looking into his eyes, "We've a fair way to go to make this endless labor seem like anything worthwhile." "Well dear," Nathaniel answers, "There's a bountiful world around us and once we carve our place in it we'll be more than rewarded for our efforts. This land is a gold mine, just waiting to be harvested. The Lord led us to this place, and I know he'll help us build a new Zion in the new world."

"We cut another beauty today, should fetch more than a fair price at market." he adds. "That wouldn't be another King's Pine would it?" asks Rebecca. "Never saw a mark," answers Nathaniel, raising his eyes "The King's Surveyors must have missed another one." he adds with a smile. Rebecca answers sternly, "Well, I hope you're right. We don't want the Governor or his troops interfering with our land grant."

Nathaniel retorts as he gazes back into her worried eyes, "Our grant was fought and paid for when we won the last war. It's the only pay I ever received for beating back the French and the Indians, and I lost a lot of good friends in that war fighting for the bloody British crown as well!"

Rebecca answers soothingly, "Now, now, Nathaniel, let's not get riled up again about that bloody war. The mutton stew's ready, and I think you at least owe your son a decent meal after all of his hard labor." As the last rays of sun vanish from the sky, and firelight fills the darkening room, they bless their food and silently start eating their evening meal.

After dinner, Nathaniel pulls out his Bible and starts reading to his family as they sit by the fire. "You are the light of the world. A city that is set on a hill cannot be hidden. Nor do they light a lamp and put it under a basket, but on a lamp stand, and it gives light to all who are in the house. Let your light so shine before men, that they may see your good works and glorify your Father in heaven." He quotes, and puts his Bible down. "As my father before me, and his father before him, we are set upon this mission: To tame this wilderness and civilize it in the name of God."

"The reason we fought the Indians and the French in that war was so that we could claim this land from the natives and build homes here for ourselves and our families. Gone are the towns and commons of our former lands. Here we have an opportunity to create new towns like the ones we started in Massachusetts and build a successful future for our families and our future generations."

"The towering pine we took down today shows what we can

achieve if we pull together as a team. I think now we should thank God for our successes. Let us pray: "Dear Lord, since we came to this wilderness of New Hampshire, I know matters have been much more difficult than they were for us in the Colony of Massachusetts. Your Divine providence has brought us here safely. As your humble servants we are carrying out your work, and spreading your word across this untamed land. Help us to succeed in fulfilling your wishes, and bless us as we go about our daily work. In Jesus' name we pray. Amen." "Amen." The family replies in unison. "Now we'd better get to bed, we've a hard day tomorrow. Goodnight little ones." "Good night father." Ben answers as he carries little Katherine off to bed.

As Rebecca tucks the children to bed she thinks back to the town commons and churches of Massachusetts, and how uncivilized and wild the woods of New Hampshire now seemed. "Nathaniel," she speaks softly, " Do you think we've made the right choice in coming to these parts? Tomorrow some stray savages, with a grudge against Englishmen, could reign down upon us and we'd never be heard from again."

"There, there, Rebecca," Nathaniel speaks reassuringly, "My musket will take care of the lot of their bows and arrows, and we're well fortified inside this cabin. Besides, Jacques Pierre and his boys are due by in two days on their trader's route. If there's anything amiss in the valley, surely they'll spread the word and we'll rout any stray savages the way we did in back in '60. The Indians and French have turned tail and run by law of the Treaty, and this land is ours." He pauses, "We'll make of it what we can." "I hope so" Rebecca replies worriedly as they lay down for the night, "I do miss my friends back home, and these cabin walls seem a pretty thin comfort, compared to the voices and busy sounds of our former town."

Nathaniel reflects for a moment then says, "Tomorrow, we'll

finish limbing our new prize, and it'll be ready to be sawn or taken to market. A few more of these big pines, and we'll have cut enough to buy plenty of seed and other needed supplies to see us through the next growing season. The Abenaki are long gone, so let's not concern ourselves with the past, and focus on the bright future in the new life we're beginning here."

"Agreed," says Rebecca smilingly, "I'm just worried about our safety, and I do keep hearing those voices from home from those who warned us about coming to the untamed north." Looking over at Nathaniel she sees that he's fallen asleep after the hard day's work. Her eyes close as she gives in to sleep listening to the ancient river's flow.

Chapter 2

As the sun's early rays begin to light and disperse the morning mist, the pristine New England forest comes alive. In a vista that has gone untouched for thousands of years, the ancient towering trees appear to shine, as their leaves become lit like jewels by the sun in the early morning dew. The sounds of seemingly endless numbers of birds and forest animals grow and rise with the sun as it has for eons before. The wildlife's seeming conversations fill the air more and more until they eventually become unnoticed as another routine part of the woodland day. Eventually as the darkness gives way to sunlight, it also disperses the dark and brings in the hope and promise of a new wilderness day.

Rebecca wakes to these familiar morning sounds, and stretches and yawns as she rises out of bed. She now feels serenity in the place, and gone are her fears from the night before. The scene envelops her, and she is now looking forward to her day surrounded by the wonders of this new world. She gets up, puts on her morning coat, and stokes the embers of the fire built the previous night, as she begins to prepares fresh johnnycakes and smoked sausage for the family's morning meal.

The sound of her morning activities arouses Nathaniel, who rubs his eyes and sits up in bed. "With all of this racket, I thought a bear had stumbled into the cabin again." He says, as he grins and gets out of bed. " No, no bear this time, my dear." Rebecca smilingly replies as she recalls the morning a fortnight before when she forgot to latch the cabin door. "I was surprised that big old bear didn't have us for breakfast that morning."

Nathaniel answers sleepily, "No, they're basically a tame animal, lest they're aroused. He was just looking for his breakfast, and he appeared to take a liking to your johnnycakes." Rebecca answers insolently. "I'm not making johnnycakes or anything for the wild creatures around here. Come now and eat your breakfast before it gets cold."

Ben wakes up and walks to the table drowsily. "I'm so hungry I could eat a horse." He sleepily says with a yawn. Rebecca smiles and says, "Well the way you've been eating lately, we may have to slaughter one of the horses to fill that belly of yours. Luckily there's plenty of game in these parts, and I don't think it will ever come to that."

Nathaniel interjects as he eats his corn meal breakfast trying to put his wife's fears to rest, "Ayuh, looks like we're living the American dream out here in the northern woods. Paradise on earth, and we're the blessed ones." Rebecca replies apologetically while pouring him some more tea, "Now, now Nathaniel. I wouldn't go that far, but the morning light does provide a better view of things... Things do look better in the morning, but we'd better get on with our chores, lest we waste a beautiful day."

Sensing an opportunity to move on to today's chores, Nathaniel quickly smiles and instructs his son. "Now you'd best tend to the livestock, Ben. I'll tackle that pine we cut yesterday. You can come and join me when you're done with the animals." He pauses and adds, hinting to his wife, "and I'll bet there's picking to be done in the garden as well." "I'll tend to the garden," Says Rebecca, "and we'll have a fine pease porridge for dinner. We still have plenty of salt pork left over from the hogs we slaughtered two months ago... But the shell beans are really coming in Nathaniel, and I could use some help picking today, if you men aren't to busy trying to chop down the whole forest."

Nathaniel replies, "Well, I didn't think we could chop down the *whole* forest today, so I guess we can lend a hand at some point... and as I said last night I also 'expect that Jacques Pierre and his boys will be by in two days as usual. You can set your clock by Jacques, and for some fair trade, they'll be glad to help with the chopping, and Ben and I can help you get ahead of the picking. Now enough dilly-dallying lets get at it." He says as he gets up from the table and heads out the door. "I'll be right behind you Father, let me grab some of these yummy cakes, and I'll head out to the barn." Ben says. "Just two Ben, I don't want you spoiling your lunch." His mother says. " Yes Mum." Ben says disappointedly, as he puts two in his pocket and heads towards the barn.

Nathaniel is walking down the south trail to the logging site; he realizes that he's forgotten his musket and thinks, "What are the chances of any danger happening today? It's been peaceful in these parts since we staked our claim a few months ago. Guess I'll just finish limbing the tree, and grab my musket come lunchtime.

As he reaches the clearing a half a mile from the homestead where he and Ben had felled the giant pine the day before, he spies four riders coming towards him down the trail in the distance. He thinks, of all of the days for me to forget my musket, it would be the one day that I might actually need it. I'd better return to the cabin and fetch it before the riders reach me, and I am left helpless. He turns and begins to hastily jaunt back to the cabin, but looking back at the riders as they become closer, he recognizes them to be the French trader Jacques Pierre and his boys. Feeling relieved, he strides over to greet his friend.

"How's the fur trading business treating you, my friend? Must be good, you're two days early on your route. Too many pelts to carry on your horses?" asks Nathaniel, smiling as he greets the French fur trader. Jacques Pierre answers by leaping off his horse, and quickly shaking Nathaniel's hand. He says returning the smile, "Bonjour, mon ami Nathaniel Jarvis. As long as there are beaver in the woods and fools in Europe willing to pay top dollar for their fine pelts, we'll do fine my friend, and I can't see that ending unless the sun refuses to rise, the forests disappear, and the creeks stop running downhill."

Nathaniel utters sarcastically, "Forests disappear, and creeks stop running downhill? You're dreaming Jacques. I'm just trying to clear enough land to plant a garden size enough to feed my family and raise some crops to sell at the fort. I wish all of these trees would disappear, though it'd save me a heap of time chopping. Just carving a hole in this dense wilderness keeps Ben and I more than busy enough." "No, I don't see that happening either, my friend." Chuckles Jacques, adding, "We French have been trapping in this valley for over a century and a half, and we haven't even started to run out of pelts yet."

Nathaniel smiles and says, "No, I can't see those furry little vermin running out of places to hide in all of this, but I'm going to do my best to put a dent in these woods, so we have an area big enough for civilized folks like us to raise a family and make a decent living farming and such." He puts his hand on Jacques' shoulder saying, "Sure could use a hand though, now our crops are coming in. Ben and I are having trouble keeping up with the chopping with the extra work during harvest. With tending livestock, and picking crops, the forest is starting to reclaim what little land we've cleared. We've been stubbing what trees we can, but we're not winning the battle."

"I can't offer you much for your work, Jacques Pierre, but I can offer up some of Becca's fine home cooking, and warm bedding for the night. You and your boys will sleep in inside a warm cabin tonight, instead of trying to find the most comfortable patch of moss out there in the woods." Jacques answers with a European bow, "I would love to accept your most gracious offer mon ami, but there's another matter of urgency I'm here two days early to tell you about."

Back at the homestead, Rebecca looks over at the fireplace and sees Nathaniel's musket lying on the fireplace mantle. She walks to the mantle and takes it down to bring to her husband. She throws on a shawl over her morning coat and hurries to the front door to bring the musket to Nathaniel at the logging site. As she throws open the heavy oak door, she comes face to face with a lone grey faced Indian standing on the porch in silence holding a drawn plumed long bow. She slams the door shut as the Indian fires and his arrow hits the heavy door with a loud thud. The chiseled arrowhead pierces and comes through the door inches from Rebecca's head. She quickly pulls a dresser in front of the door to block the intruder.

She is desperately trying to load the musket when the cabin door flies open and the grey faced Indian bursts in. He takes the musket from her arms and throws it on the floor while he covers Rebecca mouth with one hand motioning for her to be quiet. Then he looks around the cabin and sees baby Katherine playing in her crib. The Indian ties a gag in Rebecca's mouth and drags her to the crib. Rebecca is so frightened she doesn't dare make a sound. The powerful Indian then picks up Rebecca with one arm and the baby with the other and carries them both out of the cabin. Not a sound is made as he orders an Indian outside the cabin to lead Rebecca and the baby into the forest.

The grey faced Indian orders the several Indians outside the cabin to set the cabin and barn's dry thatched roofs on fire with torches. Ben is completing his chores in the barn, but sees the Indians coming and hides in some loose hay, where he watches them remaining unseen. Once the roofs are lit the warriors gather Nathaniel's food stores and silently carry then into the forest. Ben runs out of the burning barn, just in time to see the grey faced Indian give a final signal to the others and suddenly disappear into the forest. Ben looks for his father, but he's nowhere to be seen.

Nathaniel doesn't know what has happened and is still talking with Jacques when suddenly the smile leaves Jacques' face and he says solemnly, "Well, to tell you the truth mon ami, we're here two days early for a reason. I've been hearing talk on my route for a while now of a great Abenaki gathering at the site of the former Sokwaki village, where the

Sugar River meets the Connecticut. The purpose of this meeting is to plan an attack on the Fort at Number Four and retake their former lands."

"Three Abenaki tribes, the Misissquoi, Cowasuck, and Sokwaki are gathering to meet in two days at the site of their former village. Every able-bodied Abenaki who were exiled to Canada at the end of the last war is joining them to help with this mission. Along their way to the meeting, they'll pick up every Indian who can hold a musket to aid in the attack. They are supposedly coming down the valley at least several hundred strong already and plan to destroy the Fort at Number Four and then raze and pillage all of the English homesteads and settlements in the Connecticut River valley north of Fort Dummer in Brattleboro."

"My sources are very reliable, so we've been hurrying down the valley to warn Captain Stevens at the fort in Charlestown of this attack before the Abenaki arrive as they'll be here soon. The Lake Champlain Abenaki, the Missisquoi tribe, is coming down the Crown Point Road to meet the combined northern Connecticut River Abenaki, the Cowasuck and the Sokwaki tribes, who are coming down the Connecticut River by canoe as we speak. These two groups of Abenaki are as different as their two chiefs."

"The first, Chief Grey Lock of the Missisquoi, is a descendant of the Pocumtuck tribe. They've been sworn enemies of English settlers in this valley since the English settled at Deerfield in 1670. I'm sure you've heard stories of the famous French and Indian Deerfield raid of 1704 by the Pocumtuck tribe where many English were killed or captured and sold as slaves in Canada."

"Grey Lock continued the Pocumtuck practices back in the 1720's and raided English settlements during the Indian war in this valley. He was so successful that some call that war the Grey Lock War by his name. Grey Lock was exiled to the town of Missisquoi at the northern end of

Lake Champlain for many years after the war but still led more daring raids against the settlers. Though he was a known enemy of the English, he was never captured, and his band of savages took many a settler's heads until his death in 1750."

"His son has taken his late father's name, Wawanolet or Grey Lock, to instill fear into the hearts of the English settlers, and to carry on his father's legacy. If his son is leading the attack the English here can expect no warning of an attack and especially no mercy."

"The second, Chief Metallak of the Cowasuck tribe, however, has always been known for seeking peaceful solutions with the English. He's been helping the English settlers for years. I know if the English hadn't taken his sacred region of Cowass in northern New Hampshire, he would not be joining in the attack. He's a reasonable man and Captain Stevens knows him well. If there's a peaceful solution to all of this Metallak will do his utmost to find it. It's quite a contrast, these two leaders, yet they are united in this cause for the sake of their people. If they're able to take the fort, they'll raid every English settler in the Connecticut River valley until the English have been driven out of their homesteads from Canada to Massachusetts."

Nathaniel looks at Jacques in amazement and says, "An attack at Number Four? Grey Lock? I've heard his name. It still brings fear among the old settlers around here from his lightning quick strikes in the area way back in the twenties. He was one of the most successful Indian raiders New England has ever known. Back then, he would appear from nowhere, attack settlers, raze and pillage their homesteads, and then vanish back into the forest like a ghost. The old Grey Lock did refuse to sign the treaty with the English of 1726 ending that war, and if his son has taken his name, and is coming back, I'll wager he's coming back for revenge."

"As far as an attack at Number Four, there hasn't been an attack here since Captain Phineas Stevens sent them running back in '47. Old Captain Stevens is still commanding the fort, and has remained as tough as nails on the subject. He still forces the townspeople to hold regular drills as if it were wartime. The townspeople are talking of letting the troops return to their homes, and doing away with the fort entirely, as many feel it's an unneeded burden on the Colony. Captain Stevens, however, will hear nothing of closing the fort or letting the troops go, as long as Governor Wentworth still supports financing the fort. The troops have become restless as well, and have been fighting amongst themselves, due to the lack of any real enemy."

Jacques looks at Nathaniel solemnly and says, "I hope for all of our sakes that the troops are still in Charlestown, given the numbers of Abenaki I've heard that are moving in on us. If the fort is gone, the Abenaki will burn every English homestead from Fort Dummer in Brattleboro to Canada. If Grey Lock gains a new foothold at the Fort at Number Four In Charlestown, the English will most likely lose most of western New Hampshire, from the settlements in the Connecticut River valley west to New York."

Nathaniel replies reassuringly, "I'm sure Captain Stevens hasn't let his troops leave Charlestown, lest an order came directly from Governor Wentworth. As you know, Captain Stevens was captured himself by the Abenaki in his youth and taken as a prisoner to Canada. In the time he was a prisoner there, he earned the Abenaki's respect and was accepted as a member into their tribe. He learned the ways of the Abenaki very well during his captivity and was trading with them regularly at the fort until they were forced to move to Canada at the end of the war. Though the war's been over for a few years now, Stevens maintains that there is still the danger of a French or Indian attack without the protection of the fort."

"He has been at odds with some of the townspeople on this matter, but as long as Governor Wentworth stations troops in Charlestown, Stevens'll go to no ends to make sure the troops stay to protect the settlers. The new settlers now moving in here feel safer here with the fort and the troops to protect them as well. If what you are saying is true, Jacques, it appears Captain Stevens was right about the chances of an attack."

Jacques replies, "Captain Phineas Stevens is a heroic and honorable man. I've traded with him regularly over my many years at the Fort's trading post, and have come to know him well. The story of he and his thirty-two troops repelling the French and Abenaki attack in '47 has gone down in Indian legend. The Abenaki hold great respect for a leader who survived the attack of many with so few troops. They wouldn't attack the fort now if it weren't their last chance for survival. With all of the new settlers now coming to Charlestown and the area around, the Abenaki realize that unless they attack now, their way of life will be lost forever. This attack is one last attempt to continue their ancestral ways."

Nathaniel answers still in shock, "An Abenaki attack after all of these years... I never would have believed that this could happen after what I was told before we settled here. When Governor Wentworth gave me my land grant, he claimed that this land was prime for the taking, and an unsettled wilderness waiting to be tamed with plenty of resources and rewards for all..."

Nathaniel scratches his head and adds, "I guess we'll gather our belongings and pack up and head to the fort while we still can. My family will always be in your debt for this warning. Thank you, Jacques Pierre." The trader answers, "We'd best make haste for all of our sakes, Nathaniel." And with that the group makes their way to Nathaniel's cabin to bring Rebecca the news.

Nathaniel starts to walk down the trail towards the cabin, when he sees two columns of smoke rising from the homestead. He stops and calls to Jacques, "My cabin's on fire, come quickly!" Jacques shouts out, "Get on my horse! Boys follow me!" Nathaniel climbs on Jacques' horse, and the group rides towards the burning homestead site, watching as the pillars of grey smoke grow and spread into the sky.

When they reach the cabin site, Ben comes running out yelling, "Father! Father! It was a bunch of Indians! They took Mum and Katherine, set our house and barn on fire and disappeared into the woods. I was hiding in the barn and they didn't see me. It was scary! There was a big Indian with long hair and a grey face. He looked like a ghost... I tried to save the girls, but they were gone up the north trail before I could do anything... I'm sorry Father... What are we going to do?"

Nathaniel looks down from Jacques horse and says, "It's not your fault son, but we must catch them before they go too far. How long have they been gone? Can we still find them?" Ben answers out of breath, "Not long, I'd say maybe five minutes. It all happened so fast I didn't have time to help! Can we save them Father?"

Nathaniel quickly says to Jacques, "You stay here with Ben and the boys and try to put out the fire. I'll need your horse to go after the Indians. We must hurry!" Jacques answers jumping off his horse, "Go Nathaniel! Try to save the women. I'll take care of things here. Hurry, it sounds like Grey Lock has struck and he'll keep Becca and the baby captive to sell as slaves. If we don't find them soon they'll be lost as many have been before."

Nathaniel shouts, "Hahh! Hahh!" as the horse gallops off on the north trail. He rides up the trail for a mile but sees no sign of the attackers. Nathaniel begins searching the forest for sign of the Indians, but finds none. After an hour of looking he rides back to the burning homestead and says, "I didn't see any sign of them anywhere... Ben, are you sure you saw more than one Indian? I don't know how even one Indian could leave through this dense forest without a trace of sign."

Ben answers earnestly, "I think there were more than five, Father. I couldn't see to well because I was hiding in the barn, but I did hear the sound of more than one, and I did see them just vanish into the woods. They were there one minute and then they were gone... I don't know how... The one with the grey face was making hand signals telling the others what to do... You have to believe me Father, I'm telling the truth!" Nathaniel answers, "Of course I believe you Ben. Now it's up to us to save them. Stay with me son, and we will find them soon."

As the group is standing in the homestead clearing, the last burning timber from the cabin roof crashes to the ground. Jacques looks at the ashes of Nathaniel's homestead and says to him, "This is the work of Grey Lock of the Missisquoi. I know of none other who could raze your homestead, kidnap your family and vanish unseen while we were only a half a mile away. They must be going to the Abenaki meeting I was telling you about. Hopefully we can catch them there and save Becca and the baby."

Nathaniel looks around surveying his new homestead and the new life they'd just begun turning to glowing embers on the ground. He stares down in disgust and says with disgust, "What's going on here? Everyone thought the natives were long gone, and it was safe to settle here in Claremont. We've started a new life here, and now this happens? My family's been kidnapped or worse, and all of my work here has gone up in flames. I've a word for Governor Wentworth if I ever see him again... "

Jacques puts his hand on Nathaniel's shoulder and answers calmingly, "Yes Nathaniel, everyone in New England did think that the Abenaki and the rest of the native tribes were long gone. But I believe I can say without a doubt now that they're back. Your homestead was directly in the path that Chief Grey Lock and the Missisquoi warriors were taking to reach the meeting at the Sokwaki village. Now they've captured some more valuable prizes to bring there. At least we know where they're going and we'll follow them while we still have any chance. We'd best be making haste to get to the meeting site if we're going to have any chance of saving your family."

Nathaniel regains his calm and says to Ben, "You and Jacques boys round the animals up and put them in the corral for now and get them some food. Jacques and I are going after your Mum and the baby. If we don't return by nightfall, grab what bedding you can find and bed down where you can. We'll be back as soon as we can."

Ben answers putting on a brave face, "I'll do as you say Father. Please bring back Mum and Katherine. We'll be waiting here for you. You'll find them, won't you?" Nathaniel answers as he and Jacques climb on their horses to leave, "Keep an eye out for more of the Abenaki, and hide yourselves well if you do see any. We'll find your Mum and Katherine no matter how long it takes. Be brave, Ben." The two men then ride off on the north trail to rescue Rebecca and the baby as the sun continues to rise in the eastern sky.

Chapter 3

"To Arms! To Arms!" A silver haired Captain Phineas Stevens commands as he starts the monthly drill in the early morning hours at the Fort at Number Four. "Everyone into the fort, and let's be quick about it!" he adds with a feigned urgency as his troops run down the streets of Charlestown knocking on the townspeople's doors. "Come now, they'll be on us in no time, we must make haste!"

Town selectman Josiah Hubbard comes sleepily out of his door giving Captain Stevens an annoyed look as he fumbles with the buttons on his woolen jacket while grumbling, "Must we keep having these cursed drills every month? We haven't seen nor even heard a whisper of any Indians in these parts for nigh on five years. I'd like to enjoy my last few moments of sleep without being woken by your old voice every month."

Captain Stevens coldly stares at Josiah while he checks his pocket watch and sternly replies, "Better ready than dead! Now come on, gather your family quickly and meet the rest of the settlers in the Great Chamber!" Josiah replies sarcastically as his half awake gaze meets the Captain's stern eyes, "Yes Captain, we'll be there as soon as we can... But why must we have these infernal drills at such an early hour? I'd rather rush to the fort around teatime, that'd be much more civilized and would make it easier on everyone don't you think?"

Captain Stevens rebuts, "Peaceful here or no, we must have these drills at the time when Indians have been known to attack, and that time, whether it pleases you or not, is daybreak. Now enough grumbling! To the Great Chamber with you and yours!" Josiah grudgingly brings his wife and two children out of the house and they join the settlers heading to the fort.

Seven year old Hannah Sartwell wakes that morning hearing the familiar monthly drill sounds of doors being slammed and the commotion of the settlers moving hastily down the street outside her house, "Another drill father? Haven't we done this enough times already? Mrs. Perkins wants to sleep, and I must stay here with her." She states clutching her corncob doll.

Her father selectman Simon Sartwell admonishingly replies, "I know you've never seen an Indian attack since you've been born, but this is the frontier, and we can never be too ready for an Indian attack though none have come for some years. Now grab your doll and to the fort with us all... We don't want to end up like your Uncle Obediah!"

As the Sartwell family joins the Hubbards and other settlers on their way through the tall grass to the fort, Simon says to his neighbor Ebenezer Parker, "Obediah would be proud of the way Captain Stevens carries on the tradition of keeping us all ready for an attack." Parker replies, still fighting with his boots to get them on while buttoning his shirt, "We sorely miss all of the settlers the savages killed. We're better ready than dead, as the Captain says, though there hasn't been an attack in five years." Simon replies, "We sorely do miss the fallen... Though these drills are an inconvenience, they are necessary, just in case." "Agreed." Ebenezer knowingly states as they reach the fort and climb the stairs into the Great Chamber.

Captain Stevens walks to the podium and addresses the assembled citizens as they gather inside the Great Chamber, "We must maintain preparedness. If the Fort at Number Four falls, there's nothing south of us for thirty miles that will impede an attack from the French or the Indians. It's not only ourselves we are protecting by performing these monthly drills; it's the whole of the settlements in the Connecticut River valley who are counting on our readiness. While an attack could come at any time of day, and as our history has shown, most attacks have come in the dawn and even pre-dawn hours."

The Captain goes on to say, "When I was seventeen and living with my family in Rutland Massachusetts, my father, three brothers, and I were attacked while working in our hay field. My brothers Samuel and Joseph were killed in the attack, and my four year old brother Isaac and I were captured and taken to Canada. The only way Isaac was allowed to make the journey was if I carried him to Canada, which was no small task I'll tell you... We spent a year in captivity before my father was able to pay my brother's and my ransoms and we were allowed to return home."

"Since that time, as you all know, I have been commissioned many to return to Canada to bring other prisoners of the Abenaki who have been ransomed back to the colonies... I remember one time when I was commissioned to pick up a John Stark and an Amos Eastman in Saint Francis. The two fellows had been kidnapped while on a hunting trip up in Rumney. I remember this one well because of the story I was told when I arrived. It seems these two men were forced to run the gauntlet when they were first brought there. I don't know if you young fellows know what running the gauntlet is, but the Abenaki old timers lined up their young fellows in two lines holding sticks. The captives were forced to walk between the lines receiving many blows. Well that Eastman he shouted out "I'll beat all your young men" as he started through the gauntlet and was beaten quite severely before collapsing on the ground after leaving the gauntlet."

He stops and chuckles adding, "That John Stark fellow, he went next and shouted out, "I'll kiss all your women," He was carrying a pole with a loon pelt on it and the young men of the tribe hit him a couple of times until he turned that pole on them." He stops and chuckles again, "Well he beat those young ones so that he hardly received a bruise from the whole ordeal. The old men in the tribe got a laugh out of it and he was treated very well the rest of his time in captivity. After I brought him back he was named second in command of the famous Roger's Rangers in the last war and used the warfare tactics he learned from the Abenaki to great advantage in helping us win that one..."

He pauses again to collect his thoughts and says, "But anyways, where was I? Oh yes... During my time in Canada I learned a great deal about the Abenaki tribe and their ways. I do respect their people until this day. In the time before the fort was here in Charlestown, many people were murdered or captured by the Abenaki due to lack of protection. Many of your friends and relatives were victims of these attacks, and we feel their loss greatly in this small village. That is why the fort was built."

He pauses and stares at the ground beneath his feet. "I know that many of you feel these drills are an inconvenience. There was even a petition presented at the last selectman's meeting to do away with the drills as some of you feel they are not necessary. I must reiterate that these drills are keeping us prepared and ready for any enemy's attack. This small garrison of troops provided by the colony are a witness to Governor Wentworth's concern for our safety and the importance of the Fort at Number Four in keeping the colony of New Hampshire and ultimately our sister colonies safe from the ravages that have occurred here in the past."

" I am proud to say that had this been an actual attack the Town of Charlestown, we would have been prepared and any ravages by natives or anyone else would have been minimized. Now I personally thank you all for interrupting your daily routine and joining the rest of us here for the common good. You may return to your homes, and I would like to remind you all of the community harvest baked bean supper the Baptist Church is holding next Saturday. All of your donations and participation in the event are appreciated. Good day." Having said his piece, Captain Stevens leaves the chamber, and instructs his troops to signal the end of the drill and to line up in the center of the fort's courtyard.

Leaving the chamber, Josiah Hubbard pulls Simon Hartwell and Ebenezer Parker aside and says, "I'm becoming increasingly irritated by these cursed monthly drills. Stevens struts around like a peacock and expects us to blindly hang on his every word until he's finished, It's as if King George were here himself, and we must obediently grovel at his feet every time he speaks."

Simon replies, "Now, now, these drills are a necessary part of our life here on the frontier, and if I were you Josiah, I'd stop all of this complaining and fall in line." "I too, see the need for the drills" Ebenezer adds, "Now your petition was voted down at the last selectman's meeting, why don't you accept the fact that they will be a monthly occurrence, and stop all of this sniveling." He states giving Josiah a stern look. Josiah replies, "Voted down or not, I won't stop my "sniveling" until all of this foolishness is ended." And with that he takes leave of his companions and stomps down the stairs out of the chamber.

Watching him leave, Simon tells Ebenezer. "I guess he'll never accept the fact that there is constant danger on the frontier of New Hampshire, and our readiness is not optional... Well. You can lead a horse to water, but you can't make him drink. He may calm down as time passes, but meanwhile we'll have to put up with his view."

Ebenezer answers, "His view is the view of some of the settlers here, but while the majority agree with the Captain, we'll follow his commands. We don't want the troops leaving quite yet, as we and the rest of the Number Four plantation would be left without any protection without them." Simon nods in agreement, "There are always a few who won't go along with the majority, I guess we'll have to accept that fact and carry on as best as we can. Have a good day Eb, and I'd better get my wife to picking if we're going to have enough beans for the community supper."

Simon says. "Mine too," adds Ebenezer, "We're blessed with a fine crop this year, no point in letting it rot in the field for lack of picking. Good day, my friend." "Talk with you soon neighbor." Simon grins. With that the Hartwell and Parker families join the rest of the settlers returning to their homes.

Captain Stevens commends the troops in the courtyard. "You all performed with distinction in today's drill and had the townspeople safe within the fort's walls in record time. I cannot stress enough the importance of preparedness in the event of an attack. We're not dealing with an enemy who will engage us in the style we've been taught by traditional warfare principals. They will not line up and attack us like real armies would, but will come up from behind in the middle of the night even, and slit our unknowing throats. Being as prepared as we can is the only way to deter such an attack. We must maintain our readiness day and night, in order to keep this fort, the plantation, and ultimately all of the New England colonies safe from these savages and their allies. Now you all have your assigned duties, let's be quick about them and I'll see you all here at assembly this evening. Dismissed."

As the Rangers disperse around the courtyard, Corporal John Hawkins asks the group, "Drills, assigned duties, and we haven't seen a savage since I can remember. Why must we maintain all of this for an attack that will probably never happen?" Charles Killiam replies. "It's good pay, and quite an easy assignment here in Charlestown, given we haven't seen a battle since we arrived here. We should feel lucky the Governor keeps us here given the lack of an enemy. Marching around the courtyard and keeping our rifles well oiled seems like an easy way of life to me, given the alternatives."

Hawkins rebuts, "Yes, militia life has its benefits, but I do become resentful of being ordered around like sheep waiting for a battle that will never come. I'd like to be back home in Portsmouth in a civilized town than dealing with the townspeople here. At least there we receive regular news from the continent, and know what's going on in this new world. All these people care about is their bean crop, and what the weather will be like tomorrow. I signed up to the militia to see some action, not babysit."

Killiam stops and replies to Hawkins sharply, "'These people', as you call them are laying the footings for the future settlers that come into these parts. If you had to spend all of your time worrying about your own neck, and not about the happenings of the la de da's in Europe, you' be concerned about your bean crop as well, as it's the only thihg feeding you come the harsh winters around here. I'm sick and tired of hearing complaints about how boring and rural this life is, until we arrived ten years ago "these people" were being slaughtered and captured to be sold as slaves on a regular basis. If Captain Stevens wants us to maintain readiness, I totally agree with him, and if any man wants to constantly complain and bicker about it, he'll have my sword to deal with." Killiam states as he stands back and draws his sword.

"If it's steel you want, it's steel you'll have!" Hawkins says drawing his sword and charging towards Killiam. Their swords meet at the middle of the courtyard, drawing the attention of Captain Stevens, who shouts to the men, "Desist now or face lock down for a week!" Running towards the men, he brandishes his own sword, and instructs his men, "Seize them! We've no need for petty bickering amongst ourselves. I'm ordering you men to stand down now!"

And with those words Hawkins and Killiam sheath their swords, and meeting Captain Stevens, Killiam says, "I'm sorry Captain, Hawkins was complaining about all of the drills, and making insulting references to the people we are protecting here."

Captain Stevens looks at Hawkins and says, "Is this true Corporal?

We've no need for insurrection around here. What do you have to say for yourself?" Hawkins says backing down, " I may have made some remarks about all of drilling, and the lack of communication with the rest of the colonies, but we've been here without any action for so long, a soldier gets restless. I signed up to be in the militia, not a contestant in a local sewing bee."

Stevens rebuts, "Corporal, lack of action is the militia's goal. These people have seen murder, their farms burned to the ground, their loved ones captured, tortured, and taken to who knows where. The Governor had to put us here to maintain order in this valley. If the Governor wants a battery of troops here at Number Four plantation, my mission is to see that one is here, prepared, ready, and as you're being well paid Corporal, I will not put up with any complaints on the matter, nor will I put up with any fighting among ourselves, due to lack of "quote", action."

" I'm not sure who is really at fault here, but as a lesson to the rest of the troop, both you men are hereby ordered to remain in the guardhouse until further notice." Motioning to two of the Rangers he adds, "You men, escort Corporal Hawkins and Mr. Killiam to the guardhouse to remain there until you receive my orders."

"Yes sir" the Rangers reply as they start leading Hawkins and Killiam towards the guardhouse, " Now get on you two, we'll have none of this infighting around here Let's go!" Captain Stevens pauses and addresses the rest of the troop, "Our mission here is clear. If any of the rest of you have any further issues with our collective purpose, or the methods by which I am using to help us achieve these goals, address them to me personally by seeing me in my office. I will have no more of this bickering. Now let's get back to our duties. Dismissed."

"The captain is a hard man." Josiah says to Simon as they witness

the events that just occurred in the troop. "Hard, true, but purposeful
and clear. When he arrived here, the natives were running amuck among
us, burning down our homes at will, and disappearing back into the forest
like spirits."

"Those days are long gone." Rebuts Josiah and continues,
"There's no reason to keep a troop of men constantly on alert for an enemy
that will never appear. The soldiers are getting weary of Steven's constant
drilling, and myself, I don't see any rational reason for keeping the men in
the fort at all. We've no reason to fear an enemy long gone."

Simon replies, "Reason or no, the Governor has stationed the
troops here in Charlestown, and it is not up to us to question his decisions.
I've had enough of this repetitive discussion, I have fields to tend, work at
the mill to finish, and I am not wasting any more time on idle discussion
with you Mr. Hubbard, Good Day!" With that, Simon grabs Hannah by the
hand and leads her back to his homestead.

Josiah grumbles to himself, not realizing that his words are being
heard, "If I ever see any reason at all for this waste of time and effort
called the troop stationed at the Fort at Number 4, I will give away my
farm, move in with a native tribe, and live under a tree." Overhearing him
Ebenezer replies smiling, "I'll take you up on your offer, and this town
would be better of without dissenters like you. Can I pick the tree for you
to live under?"

Josiah scowls, "Enough of you and your kind, if you can't see the
forest for the trees, you are blinder than the bats who lives in my attic!"
Disgruntled, Josiah storms away to his house. Ebenezer chuckles as the
sun breaks through the early morning clouds.

Chapter 4

Nathaniel and Jacques search the north trail and the surrounding area on horseback for any sign of Rebecca and the baby for several hours with no results. The two are about to go back to the homestead when Nathaniel spies a shawl stuck on a tree branch by the trail. He reaches over and recognizes it to be Rebecca's and says, "Jacques, this shawl belongs to Rebecca. They must have come this way. We're about three miles from my homestead, but now at least we have a clue. We'll search the surrounding area for more signs." Jacques agrees and after looking for a short time they find a hidden trail leading down into a hollow by a stream.

Once in the hollow they see a wisp of smoke rising through the trees. They tie their horses to a tree and continue the search on foot. As they come to the source of the smoke they find an unseen campsite where at least a hundred Indians have made camp and are preparing a feast.

Nathaniel and Jacques watch them for a while and Nathaniel says to Jacques in a whisper, "Those are my food supplies they're preparing. The Indians must have stolen them from my homestead. Becca and Katherine can't be far. Keep your eyes peeled Jacques. We must locate them and get them out of here safely. Keep quiet." Jacques answers whispering, "I will circle around to the other side of the campsite and search for any sign of Becca and the baby."

Jacques leaves and Nathaniel moves in closer to the campsite to have a better look. Once he's within twenty feet of the campsite he sees Rebecca kicking and screaming while she and the baby are being tied to a horse. Once they are bound, an Indian jumps on the horse and they start to ride away back into the forest. Nathaniel desperately fires his musket at the horse to try to stop them, but the horse still disappears into the woods.

The sound of Nathaniel's musket alerts the Abenaki to his position and several Indians quickly surround him. The warriors bind Nathaniel's arms and legs together with vines so he can't move. He is left helpless and standing in a clearing when a tall grey faced warrior rides up on horseback.

The tall warrior peers down at Nathaniel from his horse and says to him sternly, "Who are ye Englishman? What do they call you? Have ye a name? Answer quickly and we may spare your life!" Nathaniel replies, "My name is Nathaniel Jarvis. What do they call you? I have a right to know the name of the one who stole my family and takes my life."

The leader smiles, and says to Nathaniel, "My name is Wawanolet or Grey Lock. I am the leader of the Missisquoi tribe as my father was before me. If you have information for me we may spare your life. If not you will burn to the ground on a stake or worse. So what can you tell me that is worth your English life? Think well, "Nathaniel Jarvis" if your name is so. We have traveled a long way and have little time."

Nathaniel answers, "What do you want to know? How can a poor woodsman be of help to a great chief such as yourself." Grey Lock answers, "The Fort at Number four. How many men are there and how many cannon do they hold? Answer now and we may spare your life. Nathaniel replies, "The old Fort at Number Four? That place has been abandoned for some years now. All of the troops were sent home at the end of the last war."

Grey Lock replies with scorn, "Lies! Our scouts have told us that the Fort is fully manned and well armed with several cannon. I will ask you one more question, "Nathaniel" and think well before you answer. This question may be your last... Captain Phineas Stevens. Does he still command the fort? Abenaki legend has it that this white man holds a power to slay many with but a few. I need to know if this man is still at the fort. Tell me the truth and we will spare your life to keep you as a slave to send to Canada."

Nathaniel slyly chuckles, "That old man? Yes, he is still at the fort. He is too crippled now to be moved anywhere else. He is bedridden and not expected to live very long." Grey Lock answers doubtingly, "I'd imagined that my father's old enemy must be getting old and decrepit. We will see the truth when we reach the fort. For now your life is spared. You may be of use later. But if we find your words are again lies, your life ends there."

With that he jumps off his horse and kicks Nathaniel to the ground leaving him there unable to get up. He orders his warriors, "Search the surrounding area well for any more of the accursed English, if one has found us there may be more. If you find anyone, bring them to me for further questioning. "

Nathaniel looks up from the ground grimacing in pain and says, "Look all you want, but you will find no one here but myself, and I swear I will make you pay for what you've done... Burning my homestead and stealing to my family. What have you done with my wife and daughter? You'll pay dearly for this Grey Lock."

Grey Lock laughs and says to Nathaniel, "You are in no position to make anyone pay "Nathaniel", and if we find anyone helping you they will pay dearly as well. Your wife and daughter have been taken to our meeting place, where we will meet the other tribes soon. We are sending all the captives north to Canada from there before the attack... So that was your homestead we burned today. It will be one more of many if we have our way. The Abenaki are done putting up with the English, and soon you will all pay." He then says to the warriors, "Search the area for more White men. Go now!"

The Abenaki begin searching the hollow for anyone else. Jacques was alerted by Nathaniel's musket fire and watched as Nathaniel was captured. He sees the warriors begin their search and runs back and unties the horses from the tree. He rides back down the trail until he is a good distance away from the Missisquoi campsite and hides the horses in a cave where they can't be seen. He watches as the warriors search the area but remains unseen. After a half an hour the warriors report back to Grey Lock. "No one found Great Chief."

Grey Lock answers, "Then we will feast. It's been a long ride and we will celebrate taking this English homestead by feasting here before we continue on our sacred mission. Prepare the Englishman's best food for our dinner." He says to Nathaniel, "You can watch now Englishman as we feast on your finest to prepare for victory in our upcoming battle. We have until the morning for our tribal meeting. Then you will be taken to Canada with your wife and child to be sold as slaves. Take him away!"

Grey Lock then pauses and says, "No, better yet, I would like to learn more of these English to see how to defeat them. You can come and eat at my campfire "Nathaniel" we have a lot to discuss. Unbind him and lead him to my camp fire."

Two Abenaki warriors unbind Nathaniel's feet and hands and help him stand up. They lead him to Grey Lock's campfire where they tie him to a tree near the fire. The warriors bring salt pork and other food Nathaniel had stored at his homestead to the fire and start passing it around for the feast. The hungry warriors eat until they've had their fill and begin to bed down for the night.

Grey Lock walks over to Nathaniel after the feast and says mockingly, "Ye English are not accustomed to the Abenaki ways. Tonight you will learn many of our ways. The White Man has no place in the Dawnland. I have vowed to drive you from our shores. You will become an example, "Nathaniel", as many of my people have been examples in your towns."

He goes on to say, "It was many years ago during your King

Phillip's War when our great chief Metacomet was assassinated by the traitor and drawn and quartered by the white man. His head was put on a pole outside your town of Plymouth for many years to warn of any more Indian revolts. Your head will lead our attack on the Fort at Number Four "Nathaniel", and bring fear into the hearts of the English before we slaughter them one by one."

Nathaniel replies, "You may kill me, but there are many more Englishman who will hunt you down. Though you may outnumber us now, many will come up the river valley and hunt you down if you destroy the fort. Why are you waging a war you know will only end in defeat?"

Chief Grey Lock smiles and asks one of his warriors, "What is my name?" The warrior replies, "Wawanolet." Grey Lock again asks the warrior, "What does that mean?" "He who fools others, or puts someone off their track." Grey Lock says to Nathaniel, "As my father before me, I am the spirit of the Abenaki. The Dawnlands, or the area you know as New England, is a sacred place we have worshipped since man rose above the animals. We will drive your people from our shores."

"Grey Lock has never been caught by you English and never will be. You English are weak. If it were not for your constantly increasing numbers and supplies coming in on ships, you never would have defeated us in our many recent wars. No English man has ever defeated or captured Grey Lock. You are too slow and weak and walk like old women. This time we have you on our terms, on land we know well, and help will not arrive to save your puny lives."

Nathaniel asks, "Why do you hate the English so? What have we done to earn such wrath? We've tried to teach you proper Christian ways, but few have chosen to accept the teachings of God and follow in his path."

Grey Lock speaks with anger, "Since you accursed English have landed in the Dawnlands, you have done nothing but lie, cheat, and steal from my people. We lived in peace with you for some years, then your never ending demands for more and more land caused our Great Chief Metacom, to wage a war against you that nearly drove you back into Sobagwa, the great ocean. Hundreds of your wooden dwellings were burned. Tens of your towns were destroyed. Had it not been for Chief Metacomet being killed by the traitor John Alderman we would have beaten you then."

"Your broken treaties are many. You continually push my people back wanting more and more land for your wooden dwellings. When the Abenaki agree to give you more, you take twice what we offer and then kill us if we remain on lands you agreed to let us have. Your diseases have ravaged our numbers as well."

Grey Lock walks off infuriated, and then returns to say with a smile, "We will be over nine hundred strong when we reach the Fort at Number Four. Once the fort is destroyed we will have the advantage in this valley. Your homesteads will be helpless and will be burnt one by one until we have forced you south to your Fort Dummer in Brattleboro, which will be the next English fort to be destroyed. I, in the name of Massasoit, Metacomet, and the tens of thousands of our people who have been killed by your wars and diseases, declare that the Abenaki will reclaim our ancestral lands and wipe your accursed presence from the Dawnlands."

Nathaniel answers slowly, "Oh Great Chief Grey Lock. Is there any way we can stop the slaughter and live together in peace? We English have found a bountiful land here with more than enough opportunities for both our people. I beseech you in the name of the English in the Connecticut River valley; there must be a solution that will satisfy the needs of both our people. Can we work together for both our common good?"

Grey Lock replies, "The time for talk is past. We have tried to work things out with the English many times only to be betrayed and slaughtered. The solution to this is the end of the invading English presence on our shores; only this way will my native people survive. Enough of your English lies!"

Nathaniel answers, "Maybe our peoples are so different there is no solution. Maybe you are right in saying a great massacre has to occur, and there is no way a compromise can be reached. But in the name of both our peoples, I do hope you are wrong in your ways of bloodshed. For the sakes of both our peoples, I will not stop trying to find a resolution to this. Good night Great Chief."

Nathaniel pauses and then looks back at Chief Grey Lock and says, "Wait Chief Grey Lock, there is still a great parcel of land between the Connecticut and Hudson Rivers that has not been claimed by my people. If the English were willing to grant a portion of this land to the Abenaki tribes for their sole use and as a homeland for your people without intervention from the English, would this appease the tribes and stop the upcoming destruction. I could petition the Royal Governor with such a plan and if he agrees, your people could return to their former way of life without our interference."

Grey Lock answers looking at the sky, "Our people have dreamed of a return to our former ways. We have been offered treaty after treaty by the invading English offering appeasement, only to have them broken." He stops and looks Nathaniel in the eye, "I did not want to become the scourge of the English. It was and is the only way the People of the Dawnlands have to preserve Albonak, the earth, and the future for our children. If such a portion of land were to be granted, we would have no quarrel with the English and could live side by side in separate territories with you. However, we have tried to work this out with your people only to be betrayed again and again."

Grey Lock rises to his feet and says, "Your words are lies, or another trick to fool my people again. " Nathaniel replies, "I could provide such a solution. Let me talk with Captain Stevens about petitioning Governor Wentworth for a grant for your people. If he sees the merit of such an action our current conflict may be avoided."

Grey Lock replies sternly, "The only solution to this is the death of all English invaders. Tomorrow morning we will kill you slowly and have you drawn and quartered as your people did to Metacomet. Then your head will lead us to our meeting with the Cowasuck and Sokwaki tribes at the mouth of the Sugar River and lead us to victory in battle at the Fort at Number Four as well. Good night "Nathaniel!"

Grey Lock then orders his warriors, "Bind the prisoner to that tree and post a lookout to make sure he does not escape." With that two warriors lead Nathaniel off and tie him to a tree at the center of the campground leaving him standing to spend the night. Grey Lock and his warriors bed down on the forest floor and quickly fall asleep.

Soon after they are all sleeping, Jacques Pierre sneaks quietly back into the Missisquoi campsite. He sees Nathaniel bound to a tree at the center of the campsite. With the stealth of a French fur trader he approaches the lookout and knocks him out with the butt of his musket. Quietly he walks unnoticed up to Nathaniel and covers his mouth while untying him so he won't make any sounds. Jacques whispers, "Not a sound, my friend. We make our break now. Stay quiet." He silently leads Nathaniel past all of the sleeping Abenaki to his horse waiting outside the campsite and the two ride out of the Mississquoi campsite and back to Nathaniel's homestead.

When the natives wake in the morning, Grey Lock looks at the tree where Nathaniel was tied and sees that he's gone. He shouts out,

"Where is the Englishman? Where is "Nathaniel?" He was securely bound to that tree! How could he have escaped? We have no time to search for him now. We must meet with the other tribes or all of our plans could be lost."   He shouts out to the forest, "I will find you "Nathaniel"! I will find you and *you* will pay dearly!" His voice echoes down the river valley causing the birds to fly up from the trees.

Chapter 5

In the early morning hours Nathaniel and Jacques arrive at the former homestead site where the boys are waiting anxiously. Ben runs out and greets his father as he climbs down from his horse saying in desperation, "Did you find Mum and baby Katherine? Please say you have Father..."

Nathaniel answers, "I'm sorry son, but your mother and the baby are Grey Lock's prisoners. We tried to save them, but they were sent off before we could reach them. We're going to the mouth of the Sugar River where we think they're now being held."

Ben replies sadly. "Don't Indians kill their prisoners, or sell them as slaves? That's what happened to Mrs. Johnson and she was never seen again... How are we going to save them now?"

Nathaniel puts his hand on Ben's shoulder and says, "We have to act quickly to save your Mum. Three Abenaki tribes are meeting at the mouth of the Sugar River today. From there they will send all of their captives up the Crown Point Road north to Canada. We're hoping we can reach the campsite and save them then. It'll be a big meeting and hopefully we can sneak in and out without being seen or caught."

Nathaniel looks Ben in the eyes and says seriously while placing his hand on his shoulder and handing him an envelope, "What I need you to do son is take this letter I wrote to Captain Stevens at the fort and tell him about what happened to our homestead. Jacques and I are going after your Mum. You and Jacques boys ride to the fort now, and Jacques and I will meet you there later. I'm counting on you son, can you do this for me?"

Ben answers bravely, "I can do it father, I'll saddle the horses and me and the other boys will bring your letter to the Captain. C'mon boys, let's go!" Ben saddles his horse and climbs on as Jacques tells his boys,

"Follow Ben to the fort. It is very important that we tell Captain Stevens of the coming attack. We will see you there soon."

As the boys ride off on the trail south to the fort, Nathaniel says to Jacques, "The mouth of the Sugar River is about fifteen miles from here. If we hurry, it'll take us a couple of hours to ride there. We'd best leave now to make sure we reach the old Sokwaki village site before they send the hostages north." Jacques replies, "Yes, we'd better leave now. We must make every effort to save your family before they're lost." Nathaniel leads the way and the two gallop off up the winding river trail to the Old Sokwaki village.

A few hours later, just before sunrise, Ben and Jacques' boys reach the Fort at Number Four. Ben shouts out to the lookout in the fort's tower to open the gate and let them in. They bring the horses inside the fort gate, and tether them to posts underneath the fort's Great Chamber.

The lookout shouts down from the tower, "What brings you boys to the fort so early in the day? The trading post doesn't open for a few hours. You can wait in the Great Chamber until then." Ben answers, "We have an urgent letter for Captain Stevens. When can we se him?" The sentry answers, "He's still sleeping in his quarters, he'll be up for revelry as six o'clock. You can see him then." "Much obliged." Ben answers as the boys quickly amble up the steep stairs into the Great Chamber.

Captain Stevens is awoken by the noise of the party entering the fort and rises out of bed to see what is going on. The sound of him getting up wakes his wife Elizabeth who says, "Why up so early Phineas? I've heard no revelry trumpet yet." The Captain answers, "Just a small party coming into the fort. I thought I'd get up and see what it's about. You go back to sleep dear, I should return shortly." The Captain gets dressed and walks out of his cabin into the fort's courtyard.

"What's going on lookout?" He shouts up to the tower. "An early shipment down the Crown Point Road?" "No Captain," the sentry replies, "Just Ben Jarvis and Jacques Pierre's boys. They arrived a few minutes ago. I'm not quite sure why they're here at this hour, something about a letter." The Captain answers sleepily, "Well, I guess I'll go up to see what this is all about."

He climbs the stairs to the Great Chamber and seeing Ben and the boys sitting at a table by the fireplace at the end of the room he greets them, "Morning boys, what brings you to the fort at this time of day? Ben, I thought you'd be busy at your homestead with crops and such coming in this harvest season, did your father give you the day off to come to the trading post for some candy? We have a new shipment of fine goods from Canada in. How can I help you boys?"

Ben rushes over to the Captain and exclaims excitedly, "Morning Captain Stevens... We're not here by choice, and let me tell you I'd rather be picking crops than having to flee a burning homestead... My father sent me here to warn you. Here's his letter... It's the Abenaki! They're attacking! My family has been driven off of our land and my mother and sister kidnapped! All of our possessions have been burned! We were lucky to escape with our lives!"

The Captain looks at Ben with astonishment and says, "Now calm down Ben... What is this you're telling me? The old Abenaki tribe? Here? Why we haven't seen nor heard of any natives except for strays for over five years now. Let me see that letter." He finishes reading Nathaniel's letter and drops it on the wooden floor in disbelief, asking the boys, "How many of them were there, it's Grey Lock attacking?"

Collecting himself, Ben looks up at Captain Stevens and says while trembling, "My father was captured by Grey Lock of the Missisquoi tribe himself and held prisoner at their campground last night until the fur trader Jacques Pierre came to his rescue. They were trying to find my

Mum and little sister who were captured yesterday. He told me there were something like a hundred or two Abenaki warriors armed with muskets there. He said there are two more tribes of Abenaki warriors coming down the Connecticut River for a meeting with the Missisquoi at the mouth of the Sugar River today bringing hundreds more."

Jacques' oldest boy Jean interjects, "Ze homestead in Claremont is not ze first to be attacked. My father has had word of other settlers being attacked by ze Abenaki as far north as Norwich. With all of the tribes meeting, my father figured that there will be at least five hundred warriors attacking ze fort within a couple of days." Ben looks at Captain Stevens and adds incredulously, "You have a whole troop of rangers here, and you haven't even heard of these attacks?"

The Captain answers, "No, everything's been peaceful here in Charlestown. So peaceful, the residents have been considering sending the troops home and doing away with the fort all together. You say the Abenakis have attacked in Claremont? Are coming down river, and the fort and the people of Charlestown could be next?" Ben answers, "Could be next, from what my father told me, I can say will be next. You'd best be ready for an attack Captain, because it's almost here. Don't you believe us?"

Jean concurs, "Ben is correct, Mon Capitan, there will be a fierce battle here within two days. I pray your troops are ready and the Fort at Number Four survives the attack. All of the settlers in the Connecticut River valley are depending on you for their safety."

Captain Stevens sits down at a table by the fire and says patronizingly, "Well this is a lot to take in all at once boys... If you didn't carry your father's letter, I'd think you were playing some sort of prank. We haven't seen a battle here since '47."

He goes on to say, "As you boys know, that's when thirty of us held off a force of French and Abenaki numbering around six hundred. Luckily they didn't know how few of us were in the fort and we held out for three days surrounded by gunfire and brush fire until they gave up and returned to Canada."

"Sir Charles Knowles, the Governor of Louisburg, gave me that magnificent sword in recognition of our courage." He says pointing to an elegant silver sword hanging over the fireplace. "You young ones wouldn't be playing a game with the Captain now would you? Trying to help an old man relive his days of glory? If you are, I've a hickory stick that'll teach you to respect your elders."

Ben answers earnestly, "No trick Captain. My father and Jacques have gone to the Abenaki meeting place to try to save my Mum and sister. They sent us here because there was no time. You read the letter... That's the proof! You know I can't even write yet. I wouldn't make this up."

The Captain adds sensing the boy's honesty, but still not quite believing him, "I'll have to be sure on this boys. I will send a couple of rangers north to the mouth of the Sugar River to verify your claim. In the meantime why don't you all help yourself to some candy at the company store? Did your Mum send any lunch with you? The settler's children are having a stick ball game in town by the town hall at noon. That should keep you boys busy while I investigate your claim."

Captain Stevens looks at the children who are still trembling by the fire and adds, "We'll bring you boys a hot breakfast. It's pretty cold out there this time of day. I'll tell Elizabeth to prepare it and give you whatever else you need... I'll be in to see you again once I've prepared the garrison and the citizens for the approach of the uhh.. Indians."

Ben replies, "Thank you Captain, we've been through quite a lot, and we're quite shaken up by all of this. We appreciate your offer Captain. I'm much obliged." The Captain answers, "You're a brave boy Ben, once you've had your meal we'll find some suitable quarters for you and the other boys until your parents show up. They must be missing you. Elizabeth will be over presently with your breakfast, stay warm by the fire."

The Captain leaves and climbs down the stairs from the Great Chamber and shouts to Corporal Hawkins and Private Killiam who are still in the guardhouse, "So it's action you want. Well action you will receive. Take Private Killiam and ride north to the mouth of the Sugar River. There's been a report of a large Abenaki uprising there, and I need you two men to verify it. There are supposedly hundreds of Abenaki there planning an attack on this fort. There may be danger involved. Can I count on you Corporal?"

Corporal Hawkins answers through the bars with a gleam in his eye. "Abenaki? Attack? You can count on me sir. Private Killiam and I will be off immediately, sir" The Corporal salutes the Captain who unlocks the door and says, "You can pick up horses and supplies at the company storehouse. Now off with both of you." The two happily throw on their boots run to the fort's stable.

Captain Stevens thinks, "Well, it's only six o'clock and I've already killed two birds with one stone. These men will have their "adventure" and I'll find out if this outlandish claim by the boys is true. I'd best go back to tending my duties. He orders the sentry in the watchtower, "Sound revelry, all troops to the courtyard."

Corporal Hawkins and Private Killiam ride off on the trail north following the Captain's orders as the troops come out of their lean-tos for assembly. The Captain assigns the daily duties to his troops, not mentioning the boys' claim and life goes on at the Fort at Number Four as if it were just another day.

Meanwhile, Nathaniel and Jacques are nearing the mouth of the

Sugar River when they see the Abenaki meeting. There are at least five hundred Abenaki warriors at the old Sokwaki village site walking around carrying muskets with loud war drums beating. They tie their horses to a tree and sneak in to the meeting on foot. The men are hiding in some brush by the campsite when they hear two warriors talking. "We'll get a good price for those slaves we sent north last night. The two we captured yesterday were prime. I'm sure the Chiefs will let us all share in the bounty in appreciation." The other warrior answers, " Yes, and once we take the Fort at Number Four this whole valley will be ripe for the taking. What English we capture then will fetch a prime price on the market in Canada as well."

Nathaniel and Jacques hear this and realize that they're too late to save Becca and baby Katherine. They sneak out of the meeting place and start to ride their horses south to the fort. Nathaniel stops his horse and says to Jacques, "How are we going to find Becca and the baby now? With the Abenaki attacking the troops in the fort will be too busy to send a force north to follow the kidnappers. My Becca was right when she had bad premonitions about our moving here from Springfield. I didn't believe it would cost her life." He gets down of his horse and looks at the sky in desperation with a tear coming from his eye.

Jacques jumps off his horse and tries to console his friend saying, "I have some connections in the slave market myself and know their usual routes. We can search for them later. Right now we must get to the Fort at Number Four. It's there we'll be of most use. The two of us have no chance against hundreds of warriors so we must make sure the Abenaki are defeated at the fort and then we will force Grey Lock to tell us where they took your wife and child."

Nathaniel looks at Jacques composing himself and says, "You're right Jacques, we must be certain the valley is secured. There are many lives in the balance and I don't believe they'll harm Becca as they want her to be well presented in the slave market. While the Abenaki are planning their attack, we'll go to the fort and be sure Captain Stevens has all of the help available to stop them."

Nathaniel climbs back on his horse and says to Jacques, "Thank you Jacques, I am just worried about my wife and the baby." Jacques replies, "I understand, you've been through a lot. Now let's travel to the fort. It's our only chance of saving your family." Nathaniel answers wiping the tear from his eye, "Agreed. It's our best shot at getting out of this mess." The two ride off down the dusty trail south to the fort.

They reach the fort a few hours later and ride up to the gate. The sentry hollers down, "Your boys are in town playing stick ball with the other children. You'll find the young ones there." Nathaniel replies, "They're playing a game? Didn't Ben tell you of the new Abenaki attack? Why hasn't Captain Stevens begun to make preparations for the battle?" The sentry answers, "First I've heard about any attack. You'd best talk to the Captain." The sentry opens the fort gate and Nathaniel and Jacques ride inside.

Once inside they ride directly to Captain Stevens' office and jump off their horses. Tying their horses to the hitching post, they quickly walk to the Captain's office flinging the door wide open. Nathaniel enters the office and angrily asks the Captain, "Didn't my son give you my letter? There's a large force of Abenaki preparing to attack this fort and you're acting like it's tea time. Shouldn't the troops be preparing for battle?"

The Captain drops his cup of tea and jumps up from his desk chair and says to Nathaniel astonished, "You mean those children were telling the truth? I didn't quite believe their outlandish story, though I sent two Rangers north to check it out and be sure."

Nathaniel replies urgently, "You'd best believe it's true Captain.

We just left the mouth of the Sugar River and there are several hundred Abenaki warriors there preparing for battle. We'd best do the same here as they'll be on us in no time and the entire valley will be lost."

The Captain puts on his hat and sword and prepares to rush out of the door saying, "And I thought those children were playing a trick on an old man. Trying to bring back my glory days... You're right Nathaniel. We'd best get the garrison and the town prepared for an attack. I should have believed your son and I pray we're not too late."

The Captain strides out of the office door and quickly commands his troops, "To Arms! To Arms! All troops front and center immediately! This is not a drill! I repeat this is not a drill!" The troops come out of their quarters and assemble in the center of the courtyard.

The Captain addresses the assembled troops with Nathaniel and Jacques by his side, "Gentlemen, I know we've been drilling for a few years now, but I cannot stress to you enough that this is not a drill. These men have brought me some distressing news... Several English settlers have been recently attacked up north in the Connecticut River valley. Homesteads have been razed, and a new advance from our thought to be forgotten enemies, the Abenaki, has already killed many settlers. Sound the alarm to warn the townspeople, and have them bring their necessary belongings and come to the fort. As God is my witness, we must move rapidly to prepare for the worse. Move now!"

A Ranger steps forward from the line of troops and turns and addresses the Captain. "Sir, with all due respect, we're tiring of this charade you have that there's any chance of danger from this long forgotten tribe of natives. Whatever this man has told you, there's little if any chance of the beaten nation of Abenakis ever regrouping and presenting any danger to the town of Charlestown again. I move we send a party north to investigate his claims and be certain that this isn't just an overworked settler crying wolf."

Captain Stevens sternly replies, "I've done so already Ranger. Return to the line immediately, or you'll be up for treason, and I'll see to it you spend the rest of your term in the guardhouse. We must prepare for any eventuality that may cause harm to our outpost and the citizens of this town. This is our duty and our sacred honor. We are stationed here in Charlestown to protect this town, our colony, and if we don't stop the Abenaki advance here, it's fifty miles to the next fort down the river and many settlers in between lives in between will be lost."

"I'll hear no more of any grumbling in the ranks, and we'd best get all of the towns people inside the fort before there's any more slaughter in this plantation. To Arms! To Arms! All Rangers report to me for assignment!"

Captain Stevens gives the troops their assignments and having received them, the troops hurry to their assigned posts on the watchtower and around the stockade. Two Rangers mount up and ride out south to sound the alert to the garrison at Fort Dummer. The church bell begins to clang as the remaining troops rush into town to assemble the townspeople.

Captain Stevens climbs to the Great Chamber to address Nathaniel, Jacques, and the boys who are finishing their breakfast. Captain Stevens reflects and says to the boys, "I guess you weren't telling me an old wives tale about the attack. I should have believed you boys from the beginning. My apologies."

He then addresses Nathaniel and Jacques saying, "I'm glad you survived this vicious attack from our old foes the Abenaki. I've sent messengers out to warn the rest of the colony and request reinforcements. We can only pray that some help will arrive in time."

"I haven't forgotten about Becca and baby Katherine. It's been many years since the Abenaki kidnapped anyone in this valley. It was the reason this fort existed in the first place, and it is my sworn duty to make sure all the settlers are safe. Rest assured Nathaniel that we will make every effort to find them and bring them back safely before they reach Canada. You have my word on it."

Nathaniel looks at Stevens and replies, "Thank you Captain. We appreciate any help you can give us. If we weren't under the threat of attack now I'd be searching for them myself."

Captain Stevens replies, "I appreciate your help. We may be small in number, but we will make up for our lack of numbers by our commitment to purpose. The enemy could be upon us by nightfall. We will prepare the townspeople for such an attack, and gather them here in the fort until any chance of danger is over. I must go and make sure the fort is prepared. Good day and God bless you for this warning.

Chapter 6

Chief Metallak surveys the Abenaki campsite at the mouth of the Sugar River watching as the Cowasuck and Sokwaki warriors set up weirs and spear the plentiful salmon and trout in the late afternoon. He thinks back to the time before the war with the English when this ground was a thriving Abenaki settlement for several thousands of years.

The Sokwaki tribe had flourished at the mouth of this river where fish and game has been abundant since the dawn of time. This land was sacred ground then and we thought those days would never end. Now we are forced to return to our former homeland as refugees on our own soil.

The English settlers continually push further into the lands we were granted by their own treaty. We agreed to honor the treaties we signed with them only to have them continually break their own word. They hold no respect for the People of the Dawnlands, and treat us as if we are an inferior race who is only in the way of their so-called progress.

The English settlers are a wasteful people. They kill the sacred animals, and then use only portions of them while throwing the rest away leaving the remains to rot on the ground. They cut down the ancient trees to build their dwellings or send them floating down the rivers to the sea for personal gain. They murder our people with their diseases and muskets. Our brothers and sisters from the tribes to the south that have been driven off of their lands and forced to move in to our remaining villages in Canada. With more and more people on our lesser lands, it is becoming much more difficult to find food and other necessary things to support the added burdens.

The People of the Dawnlands are a peaceful people. For many years we paid tribute to the bloody Iroquois tribe to the west to stay at peace with them and keep our lands. These white men have agreed many times over the years to let us stay on our lands and still invade them with no regard for our people or honoring their word.

We are not a warring people, but if war is necessary to protect our sacred lands, then war it will be. I have talked several times, years ago, with their Captain Stevens who is the leader of the fort they call number four while we traded with them. He seems like an honorable man. I hope he listens to the great chiefs and the united tribes when we show up at his fort in great numbers, and ask him to remove the settlers from our former lands.

We are very tired of warring with the white man. We have tried to make peaceful settlements with them so we can both continue to exist in the Dawnlands. The white settlers are growing rapidly in number while our people's numbers continue to fall. We cannot survive while we watch our lands continue to disappear. If the Abenaki are forced into war then so be it.

As the sun begins to set in the western sky, Chief Grey Lock and the Mississquoi warriors arrive on horseback. Dressed in bright red Abenaki regalia, Chief Metallak meets them with the traditional Abenaki greeting and says to Grey Lock while shaking his hand, "Welcome my brother it's been some time since our paths have crossed. How have you been?"

Grey Lock answers, "I have been well Great Chief. It has been a considerable time since we've seen each other. It looks as though the years have treated you well, my brother." Metallak replies, "You as well, Oh Great Chief, I do wish it was better circumstances that caused this meeting, but the Cowasuck and Sokwaki tribe welcome the Mississquoi in joining our sacred cause."

Grey Lock replies, "May the Great Spirits guide us to victory on our mission and return the Dawnlands to its rightful people." Metallak answers, "Though we hope as always for a peaceful solution, the

Cowasuck and Sokwaki tribes are prepared to take whatever actions necessary to return the Dawnlands to its former ways. Let us begin the traditional ceremonies." Grey Lock answers, "So be it."

Chiefs Grey Lock and Metallak stand at a makeshift altar of deer and bear skins and order the ceremonies to begin as loud drumming pierces the silent air, and the united tribes start the fiery war dance of the Abenaki around a twenty-foot tall bonfire. Warriors dressed in traditional Abenaki regalia with red loincloths; red war paint and feathers in their hair begin to dance feverishly in circles around the fire following the rhythm of the drums. They pause one by one to present gifts of food for the gods to the chiefs at the altar, and then continue their fiery dance around the flames.

To a stranger, their ancestral moves seem to emanate from the rhythm of the drums. One warrior starts singing to the drum's rhythm, followed by another, until all of the warriors are joined in the melody that builds to a mass fevered pitch which abruptly ends as the chiefs raise their hands signaling the drums to stop.

When the dance ends only the crackling of the fire is heard and Chief Grey Lock speaks, "My brothers, we have come far today for this meeting and it is good to see you. We welcome you with open arms, and may our combined forces lay our enemies low when the time comes. Let us pray. Oh great Tabaldak, creator of Albonak and Gluskab, slayer of the giant Aseneekiwakw, who destroyed the animals and injured the earth, we beseech your help in our sacred mission. Lead us into great success in our coming battle, and help us destroy our enemies who would believe they own Ndakinna, our land, and destroy nature for their own purposes. We pray that the Great spirits will lead us to victory against our enemies the white men, and Albonak will return to our ancestral ways. In Tabaldak's name we pray."

Chief Metallak replies, "My brothers, the Cowasuck and Sokwaki are usually peaceful tribes. Though blinded in one eye since birth, I have become chief through mastering and teaching our people the ancient ways. What our looming battle is about is not truly our sacred land or fishing rights, it is about our people's ideals. The Abenaki as a whole believe that no one "owns" Ndakinna, the land. The earth and sky are sacred and not to be used for personal gain."

"We have treated the Earth with respect since the Golden Age when we rose from animals into humans. For many generations, since the passing of the great ice, we have kept Ndakinna as sacred and untouched as we possibly can. We have respect for all around us, and thusly our culture lives on."

"Today we are faced with an enemy whose beliefs are very different and strange to our own. The English settlers believe that they do own Ndakinna and anyone who appears on it is trespassing on their rights. The forests and wild life to the south of us have disappeared rapidly as the white man makes his advances. Gone are our confederation tribes to the south, the English have slaughtered most of them and those who survived the English slaughter are living with us and our neighboring tribes to the north. Many promises have come from the white man saying they will not claim the Abenaki and many other tribe's lands. These promises are continually broken at the English's whim. We can move back no further. We must combine our forces and repel the white invaders."

Chief Grey Lock intervenes, "My warriors and I have had great successes attacking the white man by surprise and disappearing into the forest. If we use these tactics now, I believe our forces will be victorious in battle. For now, let us feast and dance in preparation. Eat well my brothers, we move in the morning, and we may be at battle and not able to feed again for some time."

"Speaking for the Missisquoi tribe, I greet Chief Metallak and the honorable Cowasuck and Sokwaki tribes joining us in battle. Let us feast together, and have a good night's sleep before the sun rises. Tomorrow we will attack nearly a thousand strong. Let the feast continue and let the English beware." With that Abenaki chiefs leave the festivities and make their way Chief Grey Lock's makeshift wigwam to discuss the morning's battle plans. The combined Abenaki cheer Grey Lock's speech and begin whooping and dancing in circles around the fire in a more fevered, almost frenzied pitch.

Chief Metallak addresses Chief Grey Lock as they enter the wigwam, "Captain Stevens is a reasonable man. He should see our superiority in numbers and surrender the fort without incident." Chief Grey Lock answers him, "Captain Phineas Stevens has repelled such a force as ours, many years ago. The French and our people combined and outnumbered him five to one but still he refused to give up the fort." Chief Metallak replies, "That was many years ago, and hopefully, Phineas Stevens will be more agreeable to our demands now. I have traded with him agreeably over the years, and he learned the ways of the Abenaki at a very young age."

Chief Grey Lock answers, "I wouldn't be so certain of that Great Chief, Captain Stevens has been the great defender of the white man in his many years at the fort they call Number Four. I don't believe he will give up without a fight, no matter our numbers."

"We will attack the fort and burn the town around him while he watches. This time we are well supplied, and will lay siege to the fort until Steven's troops surrender, and then we will burn the Fort at Number Four to the ground as well. Once we burn the fort, all of the English settlers in the Connecticut River valley will leave and Ndakinna will become sacred again."

Chief Metallak answers, "I hope you are right, Oh Great One. If not there will be much blood shed on both sides, and we could pay a heavy price in blood for victory all of our tribes cannot afford. If Stevens agrees to surrender, I submit we will offer Stevens troops and the settlers safe passage south to Fort Dummer in exchange for his leaving the fort"

Chief Grey Lock replies, "We have the spirits on our side. I pray for victory soon, as I can't see our people rising again after such a determined effort as this one. This is the last stand for the Abenaki. Our whole way of life rests in the balance. If we are not victorious, we are certainly done."

Chief Metallak answers, "I will agree with you on that. Our people are sick, tired, and will not have the strength to rise again if we fall in battle on this day. Let us both pray to the spirits we are victorious tomorrow, and I bid you a good night Great Chief." Chief Grey Lock answers, "Good night Great Chief, and let us pray to the spirits for victory with the rising sun."

Later that night, Captain Stevens watches as his troops make their preparations for battle in the torch-lit courtyard of the Fort at Number Four. He thinks, I was right to remain prepared for attack at all times. Many thought the threats of an Abenaki uprising were gone, but I can see now that an attack on this small garrison is becoming a reality. I hope and pray that we can repel the attack and maintain Number Four and the rest of the Connecticut River valley under civilized English rule. This has become my life's work, and I'll be damned if we let Number Four fall to the savages.

As the townspeople make their way into the fort through the Great Chamber, Hannah Sartwell, clutching her doll walks up to Captain Stevens and says worriedly. "The Indians around here have been our friends. I've seen them come and go from the fort lots of times. Why do they want to attack us and make us leave our homes? Did we do something to make them mad?" Her father Simon, walking with her admonishes Hannah saying, "Now, now dear, it's not the time to bother the Captain. He has a lot to take care of tonight. C'mon let's find our lean-to and get some sleep."

Captain Stevens picks Hannah up and says to her, "I hope the Indians will be our friends again, Hannah, but right now we all need to stay here in the fort until we find out why they're mad at us. They've been hurting settlers up and down the river valley lately, and it's a lot safer for you and your family inside the fort. Now follow your mother and father into the lean-to like a good girl and get some rest." He puts Hannah down and Simon takes her hand leading her to their lean to.

Corporal Hawkins and Private Killiam ride onto the fort returning from their mission. Hawkins gets off of his horse and salutes as he addresses Captain Stevens excitedly. "Sir, we have been to the mouth of the Sugar River as ordered, and have something distressing to report. It appears that there is a large group of Abenaki gathering at the mouth of the river planning an attack on this fort. The numbers of Abenaki advancing on us I would estimate at several hundred. That is just an estimate and their numbers could be even greater."

"They were all dressed in red war regalia with war drums beating, and doing their ceremonial dances, whooping and hollering to beat all. I'd never seen anything like it. It was like they were driving each other into a frenzy. Scariest thing *I've* ever seen." Then regaining his composure he adds, "I would urge the Captain to make necessary preparations as I assume they will be advancing on the fort within a short time."

The Captain asks, "Were you noticed? Did they have any knowledge of your presence?" Corporal Hawkins answers, "No sir, I don't believe so. They were so involved in their ceremony that they didn't notice our presence. We watched them for a few minutes from across the river and then rode as quick as we could back here to the fort to warn the garrison."

The Captain replies, "Then it's true. Send David Farnsworth to Bennington to ask Ethan Allen and the Green Mountain Boys to send help. He knows the Indian trails the best and is one of our swiftest riders. Being sixty miles away, they'd have the best chance of reaching us before the Abenaki attack. Have him gather what supplies he needs and leave now, we haven't much time."

"The rest of you start digging trenches deep enough for a man to stand in leading from the cabins to the fort's outer wall. If the attackers attempt to set the walls on fire we must be prepared to bring water to the walls to put the fire out without being shot. Hurry, time is of the essence!" The Rangers find David Farnsworth, tell him of his mission and send him to the company storehouse to gather the needed supplies. The rest of the Rangers begin digging deep trenches inside the fort's walls in preparation for battle.

Ebenezer Parker and several other settlers run excitedly into the courtyard carrying flint locks and stop Captain Stevens as they watch Farnsworth departing. Ebenezer says to the Captain, "Your Rangers have told us of a potential Abenaki attack coming to Charlestown soon. You know we've always been on your side in maintaining preparedness. Is there anything we can do to help you prepare for such an event? Please let us know how we can help... The settler families will aid the garrison in any way possible."

The Captain replies, "Thank you for your support in this matter men, and for now I'd suggest helping to gather the townspeople and bringing them into the fort would be my first concern. We must keep the people of Charlestown safe. Tell them of the imminent danger, and have them gather what provisions they can spare to bring into the fort. This could be a long battle and we will need all of the supplies we can muster in case of a long siege."

Ebenezer answers, "Yes Captain, we will be more than glad to help. We will have the townspeople load their wagons with all of the supplies available and bring them into the fort as quickly as possible. It's hard to believe that this is happening here in Charlestown again. You were right in having the town drill monthly. Now I hope we can use the training to save the town from this attack."

The Captain answers placing a firm hand on Ebenezer's shoulder, "I know I can count on you men. You've always stood by my decisions, and Charlestown needs your help now. I appreciate that. We don't want to panic the townspeople. I know I can trust you to help me in making sure that there is orderly movement from the homesteads to the fort. I'm entrusting this mission to you men. Don't let me down." Ebenezer and the men nod in agreement and hurry back towards town to gather the settlers. "We won't Captain, you can count on us."

It is about ten o'clock at night as the townspeople are quietly making their way into the fort carrying torches. The procession remains silent as they leave their homes, and by midnight every citizen of Charlestown has entered the fort. Captain Stevens orders all of the settlers inside to assemble inside the Great Chamber.

Captain Stevens assumes the podium and addresses the townspeople in the Great Chamber. "Citizens of Charlestown, I thank you all for coming here and I wish this was under better circumstances. A large gathering of Abenakis has been seen not more than fifteen miles north of Charlestown. It has been determined that their purpose is to attack and destroy the Fort at Number Four. I have sent messengers out to the other settlements requesting reinforcements. I'm not sure the reinforcements will arrive in time to repel the Abenaki's impending attack. It is up to us, as it was in 1747, to hold off the Indians until these reinforcements do arrive."

"We will man every inch of the walls of this fort with anyone who is able to handle a musket. From our drills, you all know where your assigned places are and we need every able bodied man at the walls immediately. The women and children can find shelter in the lean-tos or here in the Great Chamber. Anyone with any concerns can address me directly, and I urge your utmost cooperation in achieving our goals. To the Walls!" The settlers file down the steep stairs to the courtyard and their assigned duties as the moon rises above the fort walls.

Chapter 7

In the pre-dawn hours at the Abenaki encampment, Chief Metallak calls Chief Grey Lock to a meeting inside his wigwam and advises him, "The Cowasuck and Sokwaki tribes as a whole have voted that we attempt to end this conflict with the English settler as peacefully as possible. I am here to convey that message to the Missisquoi and as is the way of the Abenaki, to try to avoid as much bloodshed as possible. We urge the united tribes to find a peaceful settlement with the English settlers, and hopefully they will agree to our demands and return to their lands in Massachusetts."

Chief Grey Lock answers forcefully, "The time for peaceful solutions with the English settlers has long passed. Many attempts at peaceful solutions have failed since the English arrived upon our shores, and the Missisquoi people say they must be driven out now. As their numbers increase more rapidly with every coming season, this is our last chance. They have stolen the sacred lands and continue to defile them by making their unmoving settlements in the midst of our best hunting grounds."

"The Missisquoi Council has chosen me to lead our warriors into battle to defeat the English, and drive all of them from the lands north of Fort Dummer. If we are unsuccessful in our mission, we have been told not to return to our homelands, but to have every one of us die trying to save the Abenaki way of life. I expect no less from the Cowasuck and Sokwaki tribes. The Missisquoi tribal council has told me to lead the war party of the combined forces. The English fear my name, and with the combined tribe's acceptance, I will begin on the battle plan I have devised to finally drive the English out of our valley. Are you with me?"

Chief Metallak replies sternly, "Oh Great Chief, we are well aware of your history and successes in fighting with the white man.

However, my warriors and I have been instructed to attempt a peaceful solution to this, and I would request that before any attack, we send a party to the fort to discuss this. As the element of surprise is no longer on our side, I vote that we send such a party. If they fail, we will join with the other tribes in the attack on the fort and the surrounding English homesteads. I honorably submit this proposal in the name of the united Cowasuck and Sokwaki tribes."

Chief Grey Lock answers reluctantly, "As the element of surprise has been lost, and I imagine the settlers are all gathered inside the fort's protective walls, I vote the unified tribes accept Chief Metallak's proposal. We will send his party of peace this morning. If Captain Stevens accepts the Cowasuck proposal, the English will be allowed to return to their former lands south of Fort Dummer in Brattleboro." He pauses and addresses Metallak with fire in his eyes, "But let me warn you Great Chief, if they refuse their will be a reign of terror brought to the Connecticut River valley like none that has been seen before."

"So be it then." Chief Metallak replies defiantly, " I will lead a party to the Fort at Number Four this morning and give Captain Stevens our demands. We will leave with the sun and will be back with their answer before the sun peaks in the sky. I bid farewell Oh Great Chief."

As Chief Metallak is leaving the wigwam, Chief Grey Lock follows him and says, ""When you reach the fort, tell your friend Captain Stevens that if he will not agree to our demands, Grey Lock will be at his door soon, the fort and the town will be burned to the ground. I will hold my warriors back until the sun peaks in the sky on this day. After that the Missisquoi warriors will attack, with or without the other tribes and we will regain our sacred lands."

Chief Metallak answers agreeing, "Yes I know Great Chief. I pray to the spirits that Stevens accepts my demands, but if he does not, the full force of the Cowasuck and Sokwaki tribes will be at your disposal by Abenaki law. The English must leave our sacred homelands whatever the cost. Goodbye Great Chief." Chief Grey Lock answers, "May the spirits be with you Chief Metallak."

Chief Metallak chooses seven of his best scouts to accompany him on his mission. As the sun starts to rise, they climb into two war canoes and paddle to the fort in the early morning mist.

As dawn breaks on the Fort at Number Four, many of the men stationed at the walls of the fort have fallen asleep. The troop's morning revelry call awakens them into the morning mist. Corporal John Hawkins sleepily looks over at Charles Killiam and says, "Indian attack, Ha! It's probably another one of Steven's attempts to keep us here in this lifeless settlement. The old man will go to no end to have his way." Killiam answers sleepily, "I'd rather wake to a wild boar than your complaining. Why don't you man your post and keep quiet." Captain Stevens walks by and says to the two men, "We've no time for you two's bickering, Stay at your posts and stay alert, or you'll both be back in the guardhouse, attack or no." "Yes Captain." the men reply.

Stevens calls out to the sentry in the watchtower, "Any sign of trouble?" The sentry replies, "Haven't seen any sign of an attack yet Captain. All's quiet here so far." The Captain orders, "Remain at your post, and keep your eyes on the river. I expect it won't be very much longer until we see some kind of sign." "Aye, Aye Captain." The sentry replies.

Then looking through his spyglass, the sentry notices two canoes coming in the distance up the river. He shouts out to the Captain. "Wait, I am seeing two canoes coming down river two to three miles upriver. It looks like several warriors and an Indian Chief. Could this be the war party we've been preparing for?" Captain Stevens answers, "I don't think two canoes constitute a war party. It must be Abenaki messengers sent to bring us their demands. Hold your fire until we find out what they want. Assemble the troops in the courtyard!" "Yes sir!" the sentry answers.

Meanwhile inside the fort, Nathaniel is awakened by the morning trumpet call. Nathaniel says to Ben, "Sure is noisier here than it was back in our cabin. I've been hearing the troops running around all night, and didn't get much sleep. You?" Ben replies, "No Father, I didn't sleep much either worrying about Mum and Katherine. Do you think they're all right?"

His father answers, " I hope and pray every minute that the girls are safe. That's all we can do for now Ben. Once this is over I won't stop searching until we find them and bring them back safely." Ben answers, "Well. At least *we're* safe inside the fort's walls, though it's a lot noisier here than it was in our cabin.

As Nathaniel and Ben rise from their bed, there's a knock at the door. Nathaniel calls out. "Come in." The door opens and Jacques and his boys walk in saying, "Nathaniel, come quickly. Two Abenaki canoes are landing on the river shore as I speak. We must see what this is about." The two get dressed and hurry out the door following Jacques.

As Chief Metallak's canoes beach on the shore a few hundred yards from the fort, the chief gets out of his canoe and leads his party towards the fort. As he comes up the hill dressed in his traditional Abenaki regalia, all eyes from the fort are upon him. Like a vision from past millenniums of New Hampshire life, he walks proudly forth to meet with Captain Stevens and his party coming from the fort.

Captain Stevens is surprised seeing Metallak walking across the field towards him. He greets him with a handshake and says, "How have you been, Oh Great Chief Metallak? It's been many years since we've seen you this far south. You've not traveled south of sacred Cowass in many years. What brings you to Charlestown on this fine day?"

Metallak answers, "I've been fine Captain Stevens, and yourself? I still remember how kind you have been in trading with my people over the many years. The Cowasuck still honor you and your men for your bravery all of those years ago. I wish it was better circumstances that brought me here today, but I am a messenger from a large war party that is sitting not far from your fort. May we come inside and discuss this matter. It is very important to our mutual futures. I will need an answer from you to bring to the tribes as quickly as I can."

The Captain answers, "Of course Chief Metallak, come inside and we can talk of what brings so great a number of the Abenaki here. Welcome Great Chief." With that the Rangers escort Metallak and his party into the fort. Inside the fort, Captain Stevens ushers Chief Metallak and his party through the courtyard and into his office. Some of the settlers are distressed to see the Abenaki warriors walking through the fort. Josiah Hubbard stares at Chief Metallak with a combination of fear and disgust. He calls out to Captain Stevens. "What do you mean bringing the enemy in here? We have enough trouble with them outside of the fort. I say we take these savages prisoner and lock them up now."

The Captain replies, "Mr. Hubbard. I recommend that you remember your place, and stay out of these negotiations. You never believed these Abenaki would return, so I'd suggest you return to your lean-to before I have you put in the guardhouse." Josiah grumblingly returns to his lean-to, but not before saying to the crowd, "Watch your backs people, these savages are known for their deception. Keep your eyes peeled, and the sooner they are out of the fort the better!" He runs to his lean-to and peers out of the shelter looking for any sign of danger.

Entering Captain Stevens's office, the Captain offers Chief Metallak a fine cigar saying, "I imagine you've come such a long way for a good reason Great Chief. I've had word that your people have gathered from all parts north and west to attack my fort. Why, after all of these years, have your people chosen to attack now?"

Chief Metallak takes the cigar and says to Captain Stevens, "The Abenaki are a proud people. Since the time before man the People of the Dawn lands have lived in our homeland Albonak, the land you call New England, Since the coming of the English, we have seen the number of our people shrink, due to the white man's diseases and your constant attacks on us. We have lost a great portion of our lands during the wars with the white man over the last two hundred years. We are seeing more and more English moving into the Connecticut River valley, and every day they move closer and closer to our sacred village of Cowass."

Puffing on his cigar, Chief Metallak adds, "Though our former allies the French have agreed to the terms of the white man's treaty and moved north to Canada, two of the remaining tribal Abenaki chiefs have chosen not to abide by this unfair treaty made by and for the white man many years ago. We have come here to the Fort at Number Four in force to have our demands heard."

"First, we demand that all of the English settlers leave the Connecticut River valley and the lands west to your Hudson River and return to the lands south of the fort you call Fort Dummer in Brattleboro. Secondly, the land known as the Connecticut River valley west to the Hudson River will be declared an independent state known as Dawnland. Thirdly, the Abenaki tribes will be allowed to claim this independent state as their own, and live in these lands without any interference from the English settlers."

"These are our demands and if they are agreed to, the force of Abenaki warriors presently approaching the Fort at Number Four will not attack and destroy the English settlements on the Connecticut River and will allow the English enough time to gather their possessions and move south in agreement with this treaty. If our demands are not met, the English settlers will be moved south to the area south of Fort Dummer by force."

Captain Stevens is stunned by the chief's proposal and says, "Oh Great Chief Metallak, this garrison has been stationed here by order of Royal Governor Benning Wentworth of the English colony of New Hampshire, under the authority or King George III of England. The demands you now make are unreasonable and I, the captain of this garrison, will not give in an inch to any such unreasonable demands or threats from the Abenaki people. We will lay down our lives defending our claims to the lands you speak of, and will force you and your people to move to the previously agreed line north of the current boundary of Canada."

"Though the Abenaki have come here in great numbers to attempt to force the English settlers out of the Connecticut River valley and the lands west to the Hudson River, our people are of greater number. I have already sent messengers south to bring more soldiers here to the Fort at Number Four to repel your attack."

"I would suggest you and your people abandon your current attack and we will let you leave peacefully and return to the territory north of the agreed line of the current border of Canada. Any attack made now will result in the destruction of your forces, and the end of the Abenaki nation. As your fellow tribes were destroyed in our former wars against them so will this combined force of the Abenaki people be wiped out as well."

Chief Metallak stops puffing on his cigar, puts it out in his hand and says, "I am speaking for the combined Abenaki tribes. We are the rightful dwellers of Ndakinna, our lands in the Connecticut River valley where the English are continually claiming and settling the land. We recognize no land grants given by any nation who does not have a rightful claim to the land they are selling grants to."

"To the north the French have given the Abenaki compensation for lands they are occupying. The French will continue to give the Abenaki just compensation as long as they occupy our lands. The English do not offer the same compensation as the French, and over the time since their arrival have continually slaughtered, stolen land, and failed to honor the treaties they have made with the Abenaki nation."

"We have not come here today as the attackers the English report us to be. We are the defenders of the sacred lands and have come to receive just payment for these lands or the English settler's removal from them. The English are a new people in Albonak, the land you call New England. Your ways of clearing Ndakinna and building permanent settlements on our lands violates the Earth and will ultimately result in wasting Ndakinna for all peoples."

"The Abenaki have lived on these lands for several thousand of your years. The land you have "discovered" and "claimed" has remained precious and untouched by the Abenaki since the dawn of time. In the few centuries the English have occupied Ndakinna south of Ascutney Mountain, the land has become stripped of trees and occupied with constantly more and more English settlers. As your colonies of Massachusetts, Connecticut, and Rhode Island have filled, your settlers have moved north, coming ever closer to the Abenaki sacred land of Cowass."

"Ndakinna, our lands are becoming less and less fertile, due to the English's continual cutting of the sacred trees. The wild game that once filled our homelands is becoming depleted more and more. If the English and the Abenaki do not reach an agreement where the Abenaki can maintain enough territory to maintain the Earth, the English will have stripped our precious Albanok of all the resources needed to maintain Ndakinna. This land will become abandoned by the English as it will no longer sustain life, and the English will move on to more fertile lands to the west, continuing their destruction until all of the former age-old fertility of Ndakinna will be lost, to the English and the Abenaki forever. "

Captain Stevens replies, "Chief Metallak my old friend. I have traveled north as far as Saint Francis many times to meet with you and other representatives of your tribe. You and I have negotiated many settlements agreeably where captured English settlers have been returned home to their families. We have traded peacefully many times over the years here at the Fort at Number Four, and I know that you to be a man of honor and your words ring true."

"However, your civilization is old and decaying. The ways of the Abenaki are the ways of the past. No longer do we hunt with bows and arrows. Nor do we live in thatched huts and sleep on the ground. By our sixteenth century, we English have become more advanced than the Abenaki have become over the lifetime of your race."

"As our muskets are stronger than the bow and arrow, so are the ways of the English stronger than the ways of the Abenaki. I would respectfully submit, my old friend, that the Abenaki leave the Fort at Number Four at once, and return to the lands we have agreed to let you keep before we unleash our cannons and destroy what is left of your once thriving tribe."

Chief Metallak rises looking insulted and prepares to leave. He turns and addresses Captain Stevens with a warning, "True, you are my old friend. I persuaded Chief Grey Lock to let me come here and offer you a solution of peace. I see now that you will not accept my offer. If this is what you will have, I am done here. I will bring your message to the tribes. You will face the wrath of the combined Abenaki tribes now, and so be it."

Chief Metallak's party begins to walk out the office door, and the Chief turns and says to the Captain. "May I remind you, Captain, that you are in the Abenaki wilderness now. Behind every tree, there could be an Abenaki warrior waiting for you. The rivers and streams are filled with fish, but they also are a hiding place where an Abenaki warrior may lay."

"The scouts you have sent south to Fort Dummer have already been captured and are our prisoners to be sent to Canada as slaves. Any other attempt to contact your "reinforcements" will be stopped as well. I have attempted to delay and stop the attack you will now be witnessing. It is out of my hands now, and you will have the forces of the united Abenaki tribes to deal with. There will be no more help coming to aid you, my old friend, you are outnumbered and very much alone."

Captain Stevens answers Chief Metallak, "There will be a battle then, and may I remind you again that you are not facing one fort on the frontier, but the whole of the British Empire. However the upcoming events result, whether we win or lose, your tribes will be hunted to the ends of the earth and made accountable for this action. So be it then, may God rest your souls."

Chief Metallak and his party are then escorted out of the fort and climb into their canoes to bring word of Captain Stevens' decision back to the waiting tribes. Dark clouds now descend over the fort as a light rain begins.

Chapter 8

From his lean-to Josiah Hubbard stares through the rain coldly at Chief Metallak as he and his party are leaving the fort and says to his wife, "We should capture those savages now, or they'll be returning to take our scalps. Their leader looks like he's important to them the way those other savages treat him with such respect. I'll wager we could save a few English scalps by ransoming him. Why doesn't Captain Stevens see this? I'd better go out there right now and alert him to this before we lose a very valuable prize."

His wife answers, "Now Josiah, I'm sure the Captain knows what he's doing. You should wait and bring this up at the next Selectman's meeting instead of bothering the man now. You'd best leave well enough alone before you get us into more trouble with the Captain."

Josiah replies, "Trouble, shmouble, if the Captain can't see the light of day because he's to busy kissing up to those wigwam dwellers, someone had better show him the light before we're all killed." And with that he runs out the lean-to door and bolts in to captain Steven's office.

On bursting into the Captain's office, leaving the door wide open, Josiah strides quickly over to the Captain's desk and leaning on it with palms down he says directly into the Captain's face, "You're letting them get away! We'd better capture their leader and hold him prisoner for ransom to help get us all out of this mess. What are you waiting for? Get out there now, before he's outside the gate and returns to kill us all."

The Captain gets up from his chair and stares at Josiah coldly. "What, would you have us all killed? If I detain the Chief, or make any moves to show we are delaying his party in any way, the warriors will descend on us like flies on a carcass, and carcasses are what we all will be if we insult their peace party."

Josiah answers, "Peace party? Those ill kept half animals wouldn't know an insult from a complement. They can't even speak our language, can they? I demand in the name of the town council that you get your troops to stop these, these... half animals before it's too late."

The Captain calmly walks to his office door and closes it. He turns and addresses Josiah. "I've about had enough of your insolence towards my office. I've put up with your complaints about the drills and such for years now, without a word to you, sir. Now the events that you said would never happen have come to be. We are in quite a difficult situation here, and you would have me insult an enemy who outnumbers us ten to one, and could have us surrounded by now if it wasn't for Chief Metallak's desires to keep the peace. It seems to me you are acting like a scared puppy. If we show fear to the enemy now, or make some bold move to capture the few they've sent to us for an offer of peace, not only will we lose their respect, but we'll be dishonoring their people and their customs as well."

"These are not savages, as you call them, but the descendants of an age old civilization who has roots deeper in their culture than our own. From talking with many of the Abenaki tribe over the years, I've come up with the conclusion that the Indian tribes on this continent are at least seven thousand years old. That would put their society as being at least five thousand years older than our own Christian society, which is now one thousand seven hundred years of age."

"I suggest you keep your comments to yourself, and bring them up at the next Selectman's meeting. You'll have your forum there, if we are able to survive the coming Indian attack. For now, return to your lean-to and tend to your family. They need your support now more than this office needs your interference."

Josiah replies sternly, "Oh, I *will* bring this matter up at the next meeting. That's a certainty. I just pray that you haven't become too soft on these, these savages, or we'll all be lost." The Captain answers hotly, "My patience with you is at its end, Mr. Hubbard. Remove yourself from my office at once, or the guards will put you in the stockade until I deem it fit for your release!" With that Josiah storms out of the Captain's office, slamming the door and hastily jogging to his lean-to.

Nathaniel and Jacques watch Josiah's exit from the courtyard. They walk over to Captain Stevens' office and knock on the door. The Captain walks over to the door and opening it says, "Come in." and the two men walk into his office. Jacques inquires, "Bad timing Captain? That man seems quite upset." The Captain replies, "No Jacques, nothing you need to concern yourself with. Come in."

He offers both men chairs as he returns to his desk saying, "Some people just don't understand the gravity of our situation." Then he quickly says to Nathaniel, "Any word of Rebecca and the baby?" Nathaniel answers, "No, nothing more. Jacques has some idea of where they're being taken. We're hoping to find her once this is all over."
The Captain answers, "I'd be sending out search parties now if it was at all possible. My duty is to protect the citizens here, and I must consider that my first priority. Is there anything else you two can tell me about this attack that will be of aid in resolving this situation?"

Jacques replies, "I'm not sure what Nathaniel has told you but I will say that you English settlers have a very different way of dealing with the Abanaki then we French ever did. The French were not looking to build large settlements in the Connecticut River valley as you do, but live more similarly to the ways of the Abenaki, trapping, hunting, and then moving on without making permanent settlements on the land."

"With more English settlers moving in all the time, the Abenaki are finding their lands disappearing. As your settlements grow, they are pushed back further and further. What you are seeing today is probably their last attempt to reclaim their way of life in this valley and I know they will fight to the death to preserve that. The Abenaki are not usually a warlike people, but if their survival is at stake, they will fight to the end to preserve their way of life."

The Captain answers, "Yes Jacques, I understand this. As you know, I've had dealings with the Abenaki since I was young and taken prisoner by them. I still recall the Abenaki Three Truths, Peace: Is this preserved? Righteousness: Is it moral? Power: Does it preserve the integrity of the group? A group that uses these honorable considerations when debating issues must be in desperate straits to be attacking the fort and giving up the peace they esteem so highly. What can we do now to preserve peace outside of abandoning the valley?"

Jacques answers, "I don't believe abandoning the settlements will serve any purpose at all. More English settlers will come and the situation will occur over and over again until the English have settled the entire valley. What I can tell you is there are three Abenaki tribes gathered a few miles up the river. Two of the tribes, the Cowasuck and the Sokwaki, are led by Chief Metallak, and will follow his lead to preserve the peace. However, the third group, the Missisquoi, normally a peaceful tribe are being led by Chief Wawanolet, who has taken the name of his father Chief Grey Lock to instill fear in the settlers and I don't believe he will listen to any utterances of peace."

Nathaniel walks into the office, and greeting the Captain and Jacques he says, "I have a plan which may help to relieve our current problems. We've been under the thumb of King George the Third for quite some time now. Word has it he's gone daft, and with his constantly raising taxes on the settlers of the colonies to pay for his wars I would have to agree... As the King and his laws come from an ocean away, he has never even set foot on the land of the New World and he has no notion of what it's like to live here."

"These Abenaki people have, however, been surviving here for untold generations. These trails we're traveling on to settle these lands were made by them and stretch all the way from the ocean to Canada. If we did not have the Indian trails and the clearings they've made across this land, we never would have been able to settle this place, as we'd have been clearing the thicket from Cape Cod to Lake Champlain."

"Even though they've burned down my cabin and threatened my family, I believe that this land is rightfully theirs, and we are actually the invaders in a land that has been held by the native peoples for generations. I ask you, who has more right to this bountiful place, the rightful owners, or the invading settlers? God knows we've killed enough of them with the smallpox and the measles. Instead of invading, why don't we try to live with the Abenaki and the other tribes and set aside an area for them to continue their ways of living?"

"When I look at England with no trees, and a constant demand for more, and this place with more resources than any part of Europe has ever known since the Romans, it makes me wonder who is on the better path, the so-called ignorant savages, or the advanced English, who are in desperate need of the Indian's plentiful natural resources to continue to build the Empire across the world?"

"I believe that our coming battle will be a turning point in the history of this continent. As we continue to push this people back, eventually they will be driven off the continent and become part of a forgotten past. I submit that we grant to the Abenaki all the unclaimed lands west of the Connecticut and east of the Hudson and leave these lands untouched for the native people. We may learn well from their ancient ways of preserving the resources that will ultimately benefit all peoples.

This continent stretches three thousand miles wide. Can't we devote even a small part of it to the Indians and their ancient ways? My plan is to draw the line here and today, and avoid a needless battle when the bounties of this land are more than enough for both of our peoples to share."

Jacques replies, "I believe the Abenaki will be agreeable with your plan Nathaniel. As I said, they are usually a peaceful people. I've learned their ways over the years and as the Captain said when their tribe discusses a matter they will consider their three truths. These ways must seem very foreign to the English, but they value these three integrities above all else, and I believe the plan you are outlining will follow their beliefs. With their own land their peace, righteousness, and moral integrity will be preserved."

"The French have been living in peace with the Abenaki since our arrival on these shores. We have respected their ways and our only want here has been trapping fur. They have seen this and it is why they allied themselves with our nation in the last wars. The English, on the other hand have only continuously encroached on the Indian's lands since their arrival, seeking more and more land and driving the Indians out instead of trying to live with them in their valued peace. Granting them the territory you speak of will preserve the peace, be a moral decision, as well as preserving their power and integrity, their Three Truths. There is great vision and wisdom in your plan Nathaniel; I think we should give it a try. What are your thoughts Captain?"

Captain Stevens looks out the window at the troops preparing for battle and then turns and speaks to Nathaniel and Pierre. "What you are saying does make some sense Nathaniel, and would save the English lives that will be lost in our coming battle. However, I have spoken with Chief Metallak and told him that he and his nation are as much the ways of the past as his bows and arrows are inferior to our muskets. As we are in the eighteenth century of our lord, we must teach these people that they will fall in line with the future or become a memory."

"I'm sure the colonial governor will never agree to your plan, even if it is for unclaimed lands west of the Connecticut to the Hudson. The idea of granting people a great deal of land when they have no way to begin to pay even a shilling for it would seem preposterous to the governor. I will put your plan under advisement, but let me tell you now, there is no possible way it would work in the modern English Empire."

Nathaniel replies, "Yes Captain, I know there will be resistance to this plan, and it would have ramifications that would echo across the empire to the ends of the earth. Governor Wentworth he would most certainly oppose the plan if it weren't for our present situation. The high and mighty King George the Third, as well, would see this as preposterous as the French and Indians were just defeated in the last war."

"These beliefs, however, are short sighted and do not reflect a view of America that will benefit all peoples. As we speak, all of England has been treeless since the Middle Ages. Southern New England is already heading towards the same fate, the natural resources becoming less plentiful with more settlers constantly moving in. What brought my family north to New Hampshire was the prospect of a better life. More plentiful forests and untamed lands where we can stake our claim and provide a better life for our children."

"Colonists are arriving on our shores at an ever-quickening pace. Our original colonies are becoming filled, and as we spread our English ways more and more land forested land becomes fields and the natives and wildlife are forced to retreat. My plan of granting the Abenaki and their fellow tribes a sizeable piece of these lands to continue living in their ancestral ways is the only solution to our living in peace with the Indians. If not. I can see the end of the Indian ways on this continent coming within the next hundred year, given the superiority of the rifle to the bow."

"The Indian ways have kept this continent the virgin land we now see for untold generations. If we ignore their pleas to continue living the way they always have, and granting them the land between the two rivers to do so, we will end up ruining the land they have worked for untold centuries to protect. In the eyes of God we will be committing a genocide on these people and be continually ruining this land until we reach the west coast."

Captain Stevens rises and speaks to Nathaniel. "Your words are treasonous, sir, and I could have you brought up on charges of treason for even speaking of such things. The English Empire will never agree with a plan that grants an area half of the size of Wales to tribes of savages, especially when there are already English settlements there. I lived with the Abenaki when I was captured as a youth. I do realize that their claims are valid, but being a British officer, I have no choice but to follow orders, and regretfully the Abenaki attack must be repelled. As I told Chief Metallak, their ways are those of the past."

Jacques Pierre addresses Nathaniel and Captain Stevens, trying to calm them down, "Gentlemen, I can see both your points, but I will have to agree with Nathaniel on this. As the English advance the game I trap and the natives who live with them are constantly being forced off their land."

"The unclaimed land between the two rivers is very hilly, and not very suitable for English farming. However, the lands to the west hold great promise for the English. It is flatter land and more suitable for the plow, and English settlements."

"Again I will say that Nathaniel's words hold great foresight and great vision. My advice would be to give the Abenaki and the other tribes these lands and live peacefully with them. You English have broken every treaty you have made with the Indians of New England, why not try to keep your word and grant them a place to live. "

Nathaniel interjects, "Very true my friend. The only large areas of land that are suitable for the plow between the two rivers are in the Connecticut and Hudson River valleys, and have already been claimed. My vote would be towards granting the Abenaki the unclaimed land in between and avoiding any more unneeded bloodshed."

Captain Stevens replies with authority, "Unfortunately this matter is not up to a vote. I am the commanding office here and will uphold the trust put upon me when I received my command. I have sent word to Bennington of our current situation and Ethan Allen and his Green Mountain boys should be on route to our location to aid us in defeating the amassed Abenaki. I just pray they arrive in time. I will say that Nathaniel's plan has some merit, though it will never be approved, and I'll send a messenger to Portsmouth to bring word of our present situation and this outrageous new plan to the Governor. Sergeant come in."

He calls in the trooper stationed outside the door as he quickly pens a letter. When he finishes the letter he hands it to the trooper and says, "Take this letter post haste to Governor Wentworth's mansion in Portsmouth. Take what supplies you need from the company store and leave as soon as possible. Give this letter to the Governor and bring back his reply. Ride with the wind man, all of our lives are depending on you." The sergeant takes the letter and hurries out the door.

The Captain addresses Nathaniel and Jacques, "I, however, have a plan to deal with our present situation with the Abenaki. Farnsworth's log sluice is a few miles north of here and filled with logs ready to be launched into the river with the spring log drive. The sluice is on a steep bank overlooking the river and if these logs were let go at the right time, it would block the river from any canoes or other vessels that are attempting to pass."

"I estimate that there are over fifty logs on the sluice and the river is narrow enough to be completely blocked if all of the logs were let go at once. Old Farnsworth may be against the plan as he'll lose all of his logs, but I think if we explain the situation to him he will oblige us. He's an old timer who remembers what it was like before this fort existed."

Nathaniel pauses to think, then looks at Jacques smiling and says, "A log jam. There is a load of giant white pines sitting atop a twenty-foot riverbank a few miles north of here. The Farnsworth's have been logging upriver from here and have piled up a stack of I'd say a good fifty logs each being three to five feet in diameter."

"The stack is held on the top of the bank by some smaller trees that have been driven into the ground to act as pegs, holding the pile from rolling down the bank. If we pulled out these pegs at the right time, we could drop the logs down the bank and into the river just as or before the Abenaki canoes pass. I believe it would make a barricade large enough so that the canoes couldn't pass. If we're lucky enough, we could hit the fragile birch bark canoes and destroy some. What do you think Jacques?"

Jacques intervenes saying, "I know the place Nathaniel speaks of. Those logs are perched at the top of a steep bank, and it's a wonder they haven't fallen into the river yet. I will take Nathaniel with me and we will explain our current problem to Mr. Farnsworth. I know the old man, and he should agree to let the logs go, if it is for the sake of the entire valley."

The Captain replies, "We'll get on with it. You two should leave now if we are going to have any chance of delaying the main force of Abenakis. Take what supplies you need from the company store room and be off with you as well. Good luck men, the whole valley is counting on you. Godspeed." The Captain watches as the men leave and thinks, it's all up to you now; we'll hold the fort until you return. I hope...

Chapter 9

Chief Metallak and his party arrive back at the Abenaki encampment a half an hour before Grey Lock's deadline of high noon. Metallak wonders how the tribes will accept Captain Steven's refusal of their demands. He realizes that Steven's refusal will mean the tribes have no choice but to go to battle. He thinks of the ways that may make Grey Lock stop the upcoming bloodshed but realizes there are none.

Anxious warriors crowd around the party's canoes as they pull their canoes up on shore. "What was the English reply?" One warrior asks. "Should we prepare for the attack?" Shouts another. "Tell us, Chief Metallak, will there be a battle or will the English invaders be leaving our sacred lands?" Chief Metallak answers sternly, "I must confer with Chief Grey Lock before I can give all of the tribes an answer. The appointed time is very near. Let me by!" The warriors stand down in respect for the great Chief and step aside as Chief Metallak passes through the crowd and solemnly walks into Chief Grey Lock's wigwam.

Chief Grey Lock greets Chief Metallak with the traditional Abenaki handshake and invites him to sit by his fire. "What word from the white man have you for me Metallak? Have the white men come to their senses, or will there be much of their blood shed in the upcoming battle? I sense you did not receive the answer you were looking for by the frown on your face."

Chief Metallak pauses, looks at the ground and says, "The English will not remove themselves from our sacred lands. They say that if we attack, and do defeat them, more and more will come across Sobagw, the great ocean, to our lands and hunt us down until our tribes become no more. Captain Stevens told me that the Abenaki time has passed, and we should leave our sacred homelands and find new hunting and fishing grounds elsewhere. I told him that his cause was lost, as we have him surrounded, but he refused to budge at all."

Metallak pauses and says to Grey Lock, "There is great power in the white men, and their constantly increasing numbers on our lands attest to that. As their numbers grow, our numbers shrink from the white man's attacks and the diseases and famines they have brought upon us by their very presence. I am not sure whether it is wise for us to attack while we have the advantage or move on at this point. What say you Chief Grey Lock?"

Grey Lock rises and answers Metallak, " We are here now, and there is no possible way we will leave without concessions from the English on our sacred lands. As my father before me, I am sworn to uphold the Abenaki traditions and sacred honor. The three truths are our most sacred beliefs. We shall consider them now before we act. Call the tribal representatives, we must put this to a vote before we act." A messenger is sent to the three tribes and shortly two representatives from each tribe arrive at Grey Lock's fire.

Grey Lock ceremoniously walks over to a sacred vessel sitting on an intricately carved birch stand covered with fine pelts. He opens the vessel and pulls out a tattered rolled piece of birch bark. He carefully unrolls it and holds it above his head in front of the assembled group saying, "The Three Truths have guided the Abenaki people since the beginning of time. Our most sacred beliefs, these scrolls date back to the time when humans rose above the animals. They will now guide our decision on this matter. He unrolls the scroll and begins to read saying, "We shall consider them now."

Reading from the ancient parchment, Grey Lock says, "The First Truth: Peace is this preserved? We have tried preserving peace with the English but they constantly ask for more land and our removal from our sacred lands. Warring is against our nature, but in order to preserve our way of life we are forced to act. If the English are repelled from our lands, peace will return and be preserved. The First Truth is upheld. Do the tribal representatives agree? " All six tribal representatives nod in agreement.

"The Second Truth: Righteousness: Is it moral? The actions of the English are not moral. In order to maintain our honor we must act to strike down the Immoral actions of the English. Is the Second Truth is upheld?" The tribal representatives again nod in agreement.

"The Third Truth: Power: Does it preserve the integrity of the group? In order to maintain the integrity of our lands, we must act against the English. If we continue giving in to them, we will keep neither power nor integrity. I have no doubt that the Third Truth is upheld." The representatives concur.

Grey Lock addresses the tribal representatives in conclusion, "Though warring with the white men is against our nature, and many will die on both sides. Considering the Three Truths has shown us which path we must now take. The tribal decision has been made and we must now repel the invading settlers as if they were a disease on our flesh."

"If Captain Stevens will not move at all on our demands, then we have no choice but to attack. We have given him a chance to leave with honor. Now he and his fellow English invaders must pay with their lives. Send word to all of the tribes. We strike when the sun peaks in the sky. Have all of the warriors meet me at the shore by the canoes. Go now." The tribal representatives quickly leave the fire to bring word of the council's decision to the three tribes.

Chief Metallak concurs, "We have done our best to avoid this battle, but our mutual lives and honors are now in the balance. We have no choice but to fight or die. I add the Cowasuck and Sokwaki tribe's numbers to Chief Grey Lock and the Missisquoi. Death to any English who try to stop us. Let the battle begin."

Grey Lock replies to Metallak, "Well, my old friend it's begun. The future of the people of the Dawnlands and possibly all of the native nations across the continent now rest in our hands. We have been continually pushed off of our lands, lied to, and been mistreated by these "English" since their arrival on our shores. Now we shall have our revenge, and reclaim what is rightfully ours. I know you prefer the traditional peaceful ways of the Abenaki, but all will be lost if we do not make a stand at the Fort at Number Four."

Metallak agrees, "We have done our best to maintain peaceful relations with the English these nearly two hundred years since their arrival, and your words ring true. Though I am a man of peace, I will join whole-heartedly in the upcoming battle. I bring with me the support of my tribes to finally rid our ancestral valley of these invaders. I concur. Let the battle begin." Grey Lock answers, "So be it, Great Chief."

As the warriors race to the shore to launch their canoes, Chief Grey Lock and Chief Metallak are waiting on the beach, standing knee deep in water to address the warriors. Chief Grey Lock speaks, "Warriors! Enter the sacred waters and stand assembled by your canoes, remaining silent." Once the warriors are assembled beside their canoes, Chief Metallak speaks: "My brothers, today we begin a sacred mission in the shadow of Mount Ascutney to save our ancestral homelands from the English invaders. The English have been on our shores for nearly two hundred years and we have tried to live with them in peace. This shall be no more."

"The People of the Dawnlands once held all of the lands east and south of place where today's battle will begin. We held these lands sacred and lived in community with our natural partners in the untouched environment that used to be. Since the English have arrived, they have plowed our sacred fields for their ever-growing fields and have forced the bear, beaver, and deer to flee to the north and west to find food. Their numbers have increased so much since their arrival that they now outnumber us."

"They have cut down our largest trees and used them to build their never moving dwellings or to sell for profit or personal gain, against Abenaki and other Indian sacred practices. If we do not make a stand at this point, here today at the Fort at Number Four, all will be lost. Gone will be the sacred trees. Gone will be the beaver and the deer, and gone with it as well will be the Abenaki and eventually all of the native tribes across the continent."

"Though we are usually a peaceful people, the Three Truths have been considered and now we must act. We must do battle today and wipe this vermin infestation from this sacred river valley to save our way of life and the future of our tribes."

"The English call us savages as they destroy all of the land they touch. The English tell us to accept their foreign values of religion while they kill our people more and more with war and disease. Today we fight not only for our people but also for the continued existence of the Earth itself. If these practices are allowed to continue, I tell you that two hundred years from now this land will have become a wasteland, stripped from all of its natural resources and the English will not stop until they have destroyed everything that stands in their path of personal profit and physical and not spiritual gains."

"We now have enough of the English fire sticks to kill all of the English invaders we will do battle with today. More may come, their numbers may become endless, but today we will make a stand that will go down in history as the last stand of the Abenaki."

Grey Lock raises his arms above his head and commands the warriors, "Let the drums begin. Let the warrior's cries strike fear into the hearts of our enemies. Let the English fear the name of the Abenaki. Let us pledge our sacred honors to our cause. Let the blood spilled today be English and restore Ndakinna from here to sacred Cowass and Missisquoi to Abenaki rule. Before any warrior enters these sacred waters, they must pledge to fight for the Abenaki ways to the death. Come now my brothers, kiss the water as you enter and then climb into your canoes to ride with the wind to victory over our foes. Let me hear your voices cry as one now as we embark on our sacred journey."

A fierce cry from the amassed warriors rises from the riverbank that can be heard for miles as the Abenaki each ceremoniously enter the water, kiss it, and climb into their canoes. Beating drums begin to sound as the amassed tribal warriors launch at least a hundred war canoes into the river. Soon their red plumed visages appear as a stream of blood paddling fiercely down the calm blue waters. Chief Grey Lock and Chief Metallak's war canoes lead the procession of over three hundred warriors dressed in bright red Abenaki war garb, as the flotilla of the Abenaki begins their journey down the wide waters of the Connecticut in the bright afternoon sun.

Chapter 10

In the early evening mist of August 25th, 1765 at the Catamount Tavern in Bennington, a group of men are discussing politics after dinner. One of the men says, "I paid Benning Wentworth for my land grant once, and I'll be damned if I am going to pay the Yorkers for it again. All of us here paid once for our grants and we'll fight for our rights regardless of who tries to stop us!" A cheer goes up amongst the crowd. "Here's to Ethan Allen! We're with you all the way!" Ethan replies, " Yes men, we've stopped those Yorkers before, and we'll protect our rights with our might to the end! Another round for my friends!" The crowd cheers, "The Green Mountain Boys are here to stay! Pity the fools who stand in our way!"

As the beer is passed out around the pub, a rider arrives in front of the tavern. Dressed in a colonial militiaman's uniform, he dismounts and after hitching his horse to the tavern's rail he strides in through the bar doors. He inquires to the crowd, "Is any one of you named Ethan Allen?"

Ethan walks over to him and replies, "Well my friend, that would depend on who's asking. If you're a messenger from the colony of New York there would be no Ethan Allen here. On the other hand if you were from the New Hampshire militia, as your uniform would suggest, then that would be a different story. I've heard of Ethan Allen, but I've also heard there's a price on his head put there by Yorkers. So what be it now? Choose your answer well my friend. There may be a life resting in the balance, namely yours." With that several of the Green Mountain men rise from their chairs, pull out their muskets, and surround the messenger.

The messenger gives a wide-eyed reply, "I am David Farnsworth of the New Hampshire militia sent here by Captain Phineas Stevens commander of the Fort at Number Four. I am delivering a letter written by

Captain Stevens to Ethan Allen, leader of the Green Mountain Boys. I have no quarrel with you sir, and if you could tell me how to locate Mr. Allen, I will be on my way. My business is of a very urgent nature, and I must meet with Mr. Allen post haste. There are many lives resting in the balance. I also hold papers that will prove my commission in the New Hampshire militia that are signed and sealed by Governor Benning Wentworth himself."

Ethan replies, " I imagine that a spy from the colony of New York would say precisely the same thing. There have been many attempts by the Yorkers to find this Ethan Allen and collect the bounty on his head. Sit down at this table and produce the letters you speak of, and if they appear legitimate, I may have information that will lead you to Ethan Allen." He then points to a seat across from him at his table and motions for the messenger to sit down.

The messenger sits down and pulls two letters out of his uniform jacket pocket. He hands them to Ethan who studies them very carefully and says, "Your uniform is that of a New Hampshire militiaman, and your papers seem to be in order. I recognize Governor Wentworth's seal to be the same seal he put on my land grants. I am however, quite familiar with the Fort at Number Four and the area surrounding it. If you are a messenger from New Hampshire, undoubtedly you would know the area as well. A spy from New York would not readily have this knowledge, and so to prove your claim as valid, I will ask you several questions about the Fort at Number Four and the area surrounding it."

"If you answer my questions correctly, I will bring you to Ethan Allen myself, if not you will be shot as a spy, and then tied to your horse and left at the New York border. I will give you a second option of walking out that door, mounting your horse, return from whence you came, and we will spare your life. Do you agree to these terms?"

With fear in his eyes the messenger answers, "I was born five miles north of the Fort at Number Four and have lived by the Connecticut River all of my life. Though your request is a risk for myself, I will accept your offer. There are many New Hampshire colonists' lives at stake, and my mission here is of the utmost urgency. Consider your offer accepted."

"Very well then, let us see if you can prove what you claim." Answers Ethan, "There are two rivers flowing in to the Connecticut River directly north of the Fort at Number Four. Can you name these two rivers?" Farnsworth answers, " Most assuredly, there is the Black River flowing in through Springfield into the Connecticut from the west, and the Sugah River fifteen or so miles north of that flowing into the Connecticut through Claremont from the east. I've lived on the east bank of the Connecticut all of my life and am certain this is true."

Ethan answers, "You are correct sir, but any student of geography would know that answer. I'll ask one more question and only a person familiar with the Fort at Number Four would know this." Ethan pauses and asks, "What is the name of the meeting room at the Fort at Number Four, and which gate of the fort leads to it?"

Farnsworth again answers, "The meeting room at the fort is called the Great Chamber. There is only one gate into the Fort at Number Four, the south gate, and it leads directly to the Great Chamber. I swear this on my sacred honor."

Ethan looks around the room at his men and answers, "Again correct sir. Only someone familiar with the fort would know this. I believe you are who you say you are, and if you want to find Ethan Allen, you only have to look directly into my eyes."

Farnsworth looks astonished and looks into Ethan's eyes and says, "You sir, are the great Ethan Allen? I hope I have passed your test, and can we move on to the matter which brought me to your door, as I said there is great urgency involved."

"Yes my man, what has brought you all the way to Bennington to seek my aid?" Ethan answers, drinking on his beer." Farnsworth replies, "Here is the letter I was chosen to deliver. It comes directly from my commanding officer, Captain Phineas Stevens, and will explain the urgency of my request." Ethan takes the letter from Farnsworth and begins to read. Once he's finished reading the letter he rises from his chair and exclaims, "The Abenaki have gathered in great numbers from all parts north and west of the Fort at Number Four, and are preparing to attack the fort and retake the whole of the Connecticut River valley."

"No wonder we have seen so few warriors at Missisquoi and the other Abenaki camps. We'd thought they'd gone north to Canada to join the rest of their tribes there. We never would have thought they'd attempt such a bold move as to return to their former lands to the southeast. How dire is the situation at the old fort, and how soon will this attack occur, and how is my old friend Phineas?"

Farnsworth answers, "Captain Stevens is well, a bit distressed with these events, but well. The fort, however, is in grave danger. There are hundreds of Abenaki warriors from as far as Canada poised several miles up river from the fort preparing to attack. He has sent me to enlist the Green Mountain Boy's aid in saving the fort and ultimately all of the settlements north of Massachusetts in the Connecticut River valley. Time is of the utmost importance. Can I count on you and your men's aid? The situation grows more urgent by the minute."

Ethan answers, "Where is the New Hampshire militia? At the present time we have our hands full trying to keep Yorkers from trying to lay claim to lands we have already been granted by Governor Wentworth. As more and more Yorkers try to lay claims to lands we have already been legally granted by Governor Wentworth, we must remain vigilant here to protect our own lands and families. It is quite a ride to the Fort at Number Four, and if the situation is as you describe it, we may not arrive in time."

Farnsworth replies, "I'm sure Captain Stevens will be sending a messenger east to Portsmouth to contact the Governor for aid soon. He sent me here because it's a much further ride to Portsmouth and the fort needs aid now for the pending attack. Captain Stevens also sent a messenger south to Fort Dummer requesting more aid, prior to my leaving the fort. We fear the aid may not arrive in time from Portsmouth as the Abenaki are already amassed a few miles north of the fort."

"I was chosen to travel to Bennington because of my knowledge of the Indian trails that lead here. The Abenaki did not detect me in the woods, and I appear before you today, as possibly the last chance to save the Fort at Number Four and the lives of all of the English settlers in the Connecticut River valley north of Fort Dummer in Brattleboro."

Ethan pauses to reflect and then says, "The Green Mountain Boys are not a commissioned military unit, nor soldiers of fortune that can be hired. We are a group of settlers who have banded together to protect our mutual interests from this constant stream of claim jumpers who come here from New York."

"I myself started the group with my cousins Seth Warner and Remember Baker to protect our land rights. I, myself have invested a considerable fortune in the New Hampshire Land Grants, and cannot afford to leave them unattended for long. I must weigh in your request for aid with my other commitments here before giving you an answer."

"As your request is very urgent, I will give you my decision by morning after consulting with my captains. As you look quite tired and weary from your long hard ride, I will offer you a room at the local inn where you will be welcome to rest and recover until I have made my decision. I'll have the barkeep send a warm meal to your room as well. Leave us now so we may discuss your situation in private."

David Farnsworth leaves the room saying, "Thank you very much for your consideration of this matter. I will await your decision. Please be as prompt as possible, every minute is critical and a delay would possibly cost many English lives." Ethan answers, "You'll have my decision as soon as possible. Corporal, please lead this man to his room."

Once Farnsworth has mounted his horse and is being led to his room, Ethan addresses his men. "Well, what say ye. Is this a legitimate request, of another attempt by the Yorkers to have us leave our homes so they can continue surveying and selling off our lands? We know that they'll go to no ends to establish legal rights to properties already bought and paid for by ourselves."

One of the men rises and addresses Ethan, "Sir, I have friends and family currently living in the Connecticut River valley. If we deny them aid, all could be lost if the messenger's claims are valid." Another man stands up and says, "We've enough to attend to here. Though I have no connections to the settlers in the Connecticut River valley, I say we should stay here and attend to our own business." A third man rises and says, "I'll go along with whatever decision you make, Ethan. I don't see how a journey to the Connecticut would substantially hurt our position here. We've enough time to spare a few weeks to help the English on the Connecticut, and being settlers ourselves, if the situation was reversed, we would expect our fellow English settlers to come to our aid."

Ethan replies, "Yes, I would expect the other colonists to come to our aid in such a situation. Though we are all Englishmen, we are not treated as equals by the English people, or King who live in England. The King seems to expect the colonists to pay higher taxes than are put upon the people of England, to maintain his Empire. There is a rising tide of revolution brewing in the colonies, and if we don't band together we will continue to be treated as second-class citizens. In this instance we are not facing a situation where there is time to confer with a King an ocean away, and I welcome the opportunity to help the colonists in the Connecticut River valley."

"Send word to all of the captains of our regiments to prepare to meet here at the Catamount Tavern come morning. We will leave a residual force of one or two companies here to fend off whatever Yorkers attempt to steal our land and bring a full force of two hundred men to the Fort at Number Four to aid Phineas Stevens and his men. Tell Mr. Farnsworth that we have come to terms with his request, and to be ready to ride at daybreak. All of you captains go now and prepare for the morning ride and coming battle. The rest of us will return to our quarters and prepare to be ready to ride come daybreak. If this situation is as grave as it appears, all of our mutual futures may depend on the outcome of the events that will come shortly. Goodnight to all. May God be at our side as we ride with the morning sun to victory." As Ethan leaves the pub, a rousing cheer rises through the Green Mountain Boys until it echoes across the mountains.

Chapter 11

It is a beautiful summer day at Royal Governor Benning Wentworth's palatial mansion overlooking Little Harbor in Portsmouth New Hampshire. The colonial governor is preparing for a summer excursion riding through the town in his regal carriage with his entourage of outriders. "It's days like these that make one feel blessed with the fortune of opportunities we've found here in the Colony of New Hampshire." The Governor exclaims, "If it weren't for my accursed gout, I would walk the route through town to address my adoring subjects."

His young wife Martha acknowledges, "Yes, my husband, that dreadful disease does limit some of your physical abilities, but I've never known a man that has gained so much over these past twenty five years as governor. Why I was barely born when you began your term. Can we go riding out of town today? We never seem to leave Portsmouth..."

The Governor smiles, "Yes, this past quarter century has been good to me. I've been able to establish this colony while making a great deal of profit for myself. My pain is a bit severe today my dear. I don't feel up to riding out of town. Maybe another day, we have a long summer ahead."

His wife answers, "I understand my love, another day... But how have you made all of these riches while those around you still struggle for their next meal? This is a poor province without many riches, yet you've amassed a small fortune."

Wentworth replies with a smile, "It's all in the trees my dear, since the King appointed me Colonial governor, and Surveyor of the King's Woods, he may have well given me title to all of the land west from Portsmouth to the Colony of New York, as well as the trees upon it. We are fortunate, you and I, and the less fortunate have helped provided me with this wealth. Now let's go out and enjoy this wonderful day. Has my carriage been prepared?"

She replies, "Yes, my liege, I believe your carriage is ready and awaiting your arrival." He answers. "Then let's be off, I wouldn't want to miss a minute. We shall go now and greet the common people. God knows they've given me all of this splendor, whether they realize it or not." He says with a grin.

Martha adds, "Will we someday take the carriage out of Portsmouth to tour the colony as you've promised? Sometimes I grow tired of the day to day and would like a change of scenery. I've heard that the Connecticut River is as wide as the Nile and nearly as long."

The Governor answers, "Ahh yes, the Connecticut is one of the greatest jewels of my colony, not nearly as long as the Nile, but quite wide... We shall take the trip I promised you, I know your fertile young mind is in need of some adventure. The Connecticut River would be the perfect place for us to go. A personal appearance would also aid in settling some of the recent claims by the State of New York on some of my land grants. It would be slaying the proverbial two birds with one stone by our excursion. First, of course, you would receive your needed holiday, and secondly a show of force in the river valley may make the Governor of New York think twice about continuing his claims on my land."

Martha helps Wentworth hobble out the door to the waiting carriage and escort in the yard. In a scene of splendor, the carriage appears to have been prepared for European royalty. The polished brass carriage has been adorned with his usual regal purple cloak, and several uniformed riders are waiting to escort him through the streets of Portsmouth. "They'll be happy to see me as always, don't forget to wave to the paupers, we must keep up the King's appearance to the masses." "Yes, my liege" His wife answers.

As he and Martha are about to board the coach, an exhausted messenger quickly rides up to the mansion towards the coach. Several outriders dismount and intercept him before he reaches the carriage. "What say ye? The Royal Governor is leaving post haste, be ye friend or foe? We have no time to dally!" The messenger answers, "I have ridden from the Fort at Number Four in Charlestown and have urgent news for the Royal Governor! Don't delay me, time is of the essence!"

As the Governor and his wife board the carriage, their attention is drawn towards the rider. Overhearing him speak to the guard, he motions to him and says, "Let him pass! What news bring ye from our western post?"

The messenger relates the dire situation at the fort, and how the furthest inland fort of the Colony of New Hampshire is about to be destroyed by the amassed Abenaki. "What?" He asks incredulously, "There hasn't been a battle at the Fort at Number Four since '47. I've been considering closing it because there's little need for a fort in an area we've had complete control of for the last twenty years. We do owe a debt to Phineas Stevens however, for saving the colony all those years ago and I was keeping it open in his honor until he retired. It really costs little more than one of my parties..."

"Those ignorant savages have actually united, and are about to take the Fort at Number Four? Why haven't I had word of this before? It's a few days ride to the Connecticut and we'll have no time to mount a force and arrive there, if the situation is as dire as you describe. What are our options here? I have many business concerns west of the Connecticut. How can we stop the loss of our entire western front with so little time?"

The messenger answers, "A plan was proposed by a Nathaniel Jarvis of a settlement with the Abenaki that may delay the situation enough to stop the current slaughter, and give us time to come up with a solution to this dilemma."

The Governor answers with desperation in his eyes, "Well tell me of this Jarvis' solution, I don't want to go down in history as the only colonial governor to lose half of his royal colony to a bunch of untamed wild beasts with only bows and arrows. What is his plan?"

The messenger answers, "It involves the unclaimed lands west of the Connecticut and east of the Hudson to the Canadian border, a portion of the lands the French to the north have named Verdemont. Mr. Jarvis believes that if we cede the unclaimed portions of this land to the Abenaki, by means of a royal grant, it will appease them enough to halt their imminent attack. As you know, my lord, this land is mostly mountainous, and holds little monetary value."

The Governor replies, "Yes, I've seen the surveyors reports and have already granted most of the lands that held any value. Granting these lands, or giving them away would not hurt my pocket, err, I mean the Province's treasury... Are any of these tracts close to the New York border?" The messenger answers, "These lands are east of the Hudson and west of the Connecticut in mountainous regions. However, there have been cases filed in the courts of both states, claiming that dual deeds have been granted to many parcels of the same land near this area."

Governor Wentworth pauses and says, "Yes, I have heard of these so called claims. In my haste to raise funds for the "colony", I may have "mistakenly" granted lands that were claimed by both states without realizing that I did so. If I do cede this track of land to the Abenaki, by royal order, how long would it take word to reach the Connecticut valley, and would it appease them enough to stop the current bloodshed to allow us to bring in troops and retake the area in the future?"

The messenger answers, "I believe so, your highness. There is a Captain Phineas Stevens at the fort who the Indians believe is honorable and they will trust his word. If he presents the royal grant to them, they should be appeased and end the current hostilities." "Well, so be it then." the governor grudgingly replies.

The governor then calls his secretary from the mansion, and seats him beside himself in the plush coach. "Secretary, transcribe this, notarize it, and have it sent to the western front with most haste. Here is my royal decree:

"By my authority as the Royal Governor of the Colony of New Hampshire on this 27th Day of August in the year of our lord 1765, I hereby grant the unclaimed land north of the border of the royal colony of Massachusetts, west of the Connecticut River, east of the Hudson, and south of the northern border established with the French at the end of the Seven Years War to the tribe of native peoples known as the Abenaki. They will have all rights to the land, trees, and any other said property within the given borders. I decree this, to take effect this day,

Signed,

His Excellency Benning Wentworth

Royal Governor of the Province of New Hampshire."

He pauses and asks the messenger while placing his Royal Seal on the document, "Will this satisfy the current situation? I've written so many grants and to so many different parties, I, myself am not certain where the actual borders were originally established anymore. I will have to board my royal coach and make my way through this new land some day to find out for sure. What can a bunch of savages do with another English treaty? We've made and broken so many with them over the centuries since we arrived here, well, that's another matter... but how can I lose by granting the natives unclaimed land that's mostly hilltops? Go now and make haste. I don't want my valuable settlements lost. God knows it's taken long enough to establish them. Send the savages west of the Connecticut, with word that if they ever cross that river again, it will be their heads on sticks paraded through the streets of Boston. That should be enough to stop this insurrection. We'll come up with a real solution later. GO NOW!"

"Yes my lord!" and with that the secretary takes the governors grant to have the royal seal placed on it and once that is done the document is taken by the messenger back to the Fort at Number Four. Little did Governor Wentworth know that he has just created a document that could change the history of the Native Americans in North America, and the course of the entire history of the settlement of United States of America itself.

"Ahh my dearest, can anything else delay our excursion? Let us leave matters of state here, and ride out and enjoy the pomp we're accustomed to. A cup of tea, my dear? Nothing is too good for my blushing new bride." His wife answers, "But what about all of the trouble that man mentioned on the western front? Shouldn't we be concerned with that?"

Wentworth replies, "Trouble need not concern us on a day like this. Whatever the trouble is, remember I can change it with a stroke of the pen. You do recall that I represent His Majesty King George the Third, Duke of Normandy, King of England, and ruler of the British Empire. I also set the record for fines for broken windows in my college days at Harvard in my younger days... Whatever little skirmish has erupted in Charlestown, I can call upon the entire power of the British Empire to crush it. Just in case, I will send two companies of the militia to Charlestown in the morning."

Martha asks pleadingly, "My liege... Could we possibly accompany the militia on such a trip? It sounds like the perfect opportunity to leave the seacoast and view the mountains and rivers of New

Hampshire... And it is the perfect season, being summer and all..."

Wentworth pauses looking at his young bride and then replies, "Of course my beauty, I cannot think of a better excuse to take you on your tour of the province... There may be an element of danger... but taking two companies of militia with us should be sufficient protection, and it is time I viewed some of my properties as well. I did keep a claim on a portion of land on every land grant for myself. It's time to see all of my assets, and you're right this is the perfect opportunity. It's settled then, we'll go."

Martha reaches over and embraces Wentworth and kisses his cheek saying, "Thank you my liege, once we return from today's excursion, I will begin packing and planning our trip. I'm so excited! I am so lucky to be your bride... Benning, my young bones are in dire need of some adventure."

Wentworth smiles laughingly and replies as the carriage starts down the street, "Yes, Yes, my dear we will go view the province... Now control your excitement, our loyal subjects are waiting... Will you please pass me a crumpet?" Martha obligingly hands him a crumpet from their lunch basket. He replies, "Thank you, my dear. Ah, here come my subjects now. Wave darling, as long as the people are behind us, we needn't have any fears. I'll have them foot the bill for our trip as well." And the procession clacks down the cobblestone streets of the capitol city.

Chapter 12

"Well my old friend it appears it's all up to us now, wouldn't you say?" Jacques Pierre says to Nathaniel as they make their way up the road north of the fort towards the log sluice. "I'm hoping so." Answers Nathaniel as he looks back down the trail. "We've a few miles more to go unnoticed before we reach the sluice though. We can't count our chickens yet."

Jacques answers, "Ahh, chickens, is that all you English think of is farming, even at a time like this?" Nathaniel replies, "I'd rather be thinking of farming than of our throats being slit by some unseen Indian. Keep your eyes peeled, my friend, or your head will end up on an Abenaki stick." Jacques smiles and replies, "You as well, Nathaniel, your head would not look as good on an Abenaki stick as it does on your broad shoulders." Nathaniel smiles and answers with a feigned French accent, "Yours as well, mon ami. Now let us ride sweeftly, ze Fort is counting on us now."

"Wait!" Jacques says as he motions for Nathaniel to stop his horse and stay quiet. "What's that I hear?" As they stop to listen they hear several riders coming down the toad towards them. They pull their horses off the trail and into the brush just as five Abenaki warriors come in to view. The first Abenaki stops his horse at the spot where Nathaniel and Jacques just were, and peers into the woods around him with his nose in the air.

"What is it?" The second warrior asks the first. " Do you see something?" "It's the smell." The first says to the second. "I can smell an Englishman coming a field away. I thought I smelled one here, but the smell is gone now." The second warrior answers, "Too much of the English whiskey last night I think. I don't smell anything here. Let's move on to join the battle at the fort." The first warrior says, "Oh alright, but I swear there are English near here. I was seeing a lot of spirits last night as well, though, it could be the perfume of a bottle fallen on the road."

As the warriors continue down the road past Nathaniel and Jacques, Nathaniel says, "Was it the French perfume they smelled? I think you should jump in a brook to wash that foul smell off of you before it gets us into more trouble. Jacques answers smiling indignantly, "French perfume? I'll bet it was the smell of your beautiful wife Rebecca that made them stop at the spot. We'd best keep our wits about us before another roving band of Abenaki cones by." Nathaniel answers as they start up the road heading north. "Agreed. I do hope Rebecca and Katherine are safe."

As they arrive at the log sluice a few miles north of the fort, they find it looking abandoned without anyone in sight. The men survey the log sluice and their appointed task of dropping the logs into the river and onto the Abenaki canoes.

"It can be done." Says Nathaniel, "The bank is steep enough, and the logs are only held by the wooden pegs on the bank. If we pull them out at the right time the Abenaki canoes will become debris floating down the river. The distraction could be enough to buy more time for the reinforcements that are hopefully coming." Jacques answers, "We can do this my friend. I'd wager the poor logger who positioned these logs here wouldn't be too happy for his loss though." Nathaniel says, "A few logs or the Fort at Number Four, I don't think there's a question there."

"Well I do!" Comes a voice from behind them. "Now drop your weapons and reach for the sky!" As the two drop their muskets onto the ground and turn around, they see three men facing them with muskets leveled at their chests. "You ain't taking these logs down my sluice till the spring log drive. My boys and I will see to that. The river isn't deep enough this time of year to carry the logs downstream. They'll all end up stuck in the mud at the bottom of the sluice. Now what makes you think we'll give up a lot of hard work so's you can have your jollies?"

Nathaniel turns, and recognizing his friend Mr. Farnsworth he replies offering a handshake, "Good day, Mr. Farnsworth. How've you been? It's me Nathaniel Hawkins, your neighbor to the north, and my friend Jacques Pierre. We met when my wife Rebecca brought you and your boys some of her fine corn bread back when we first moved to these parts. I hear your son David has joined the militia at Number Four. You remember me, don't you?"

Mr. Farnsworth answers shaking his hand, "Ohh, it is you Nathaniel. How've you been my boy? Yes, my son David is a Ranger in the local militia. He has made his father proud. Now what do you think you're doing, speaking of dropping my logs in to the river? Log drive's a ways away now. You seemed like a boy with better sense than that. What has caused you to become a common thief? You're lucky we didn't shoot you when we spotted you eying my log sluice."

Nathaniel answers, "There's about to be an Abenaki attack on the Fort at Number Four. Grey Lock has rounded up all of the Abenaki north to Cowass and west to lake Champlain to try and retake the fort. They'll be passing by your land on the river on the way to the fort and we have a plan to drop your logs on their canoes and stop or at least slow down the attack."

Farnsworth replies looking astounded, "My logs! An Abenaki attack? You must have gotten into the corn squeezins boy, there hasn't been any sign of any Abenaki since the end of the war."

Nathaniel replies, "It's true Mr. Farnsworth, the Abenaki are on the river a few miles north of here as we speak. There are well over fifty canoes filled with Abenaki warriors ready to attack the fort. Being one of the older settlers in these parts, you remember what it was like before the war and the fort when the Abenaki ran rampant through any homestead they chose and traded our women up in Canada and burned many a farm.

Those days could return Mr. Farnsworth, you mark my words, if we don't stop the Abenaki here, there will be dire consequences to face for any English settler from Brattleboro north. Will you help us Mr. Farnsworth? We've been sent by Captain Stevens himself to complete our mission."

Farnsworth looks at the ground and pauses. Then he looks into Nathaniel's eyes and says, "Those days were before your time Nathaniel. Before the fort was built, any homesteader faced the chance of being captured and tortured or worse by those savages. My family was lucky to escape, but I never told you about my wife Sarah. She's been gone nigh on fifteen years now and I still hope and pray every day for her return. She was stolen one night and taken to who knows where by the Abenaki you talk about."

"The only thing I have to remember her by are my sons, a blessing she gave me before she was captured. If you need my logs to help stop those rascals, by all means get at it. There are always more trees in these parts, but I'll never forget the ones we've lost." Mr. Farnsworth wipes a tear from his eye and tells his boys to start loosening the pins on the log sluice to prepare to release the logs.

Then, one of Farnsworth's sons shouts out, "Father look, up the river!" As all heads turn to look up the river they see the Abenaki canoes about a mile away paddling swiftly towards them. "Have you ever seen so many canoes?" His son adds, "I didn't think that there were that many Indians left in these parts. It looks like an army paddling towards us. Where'd they come from?"

The group stares silently in amazement at the sight of the amassed Abenaki paddling down the river, until Farnsworth says, "You were right Nathaniel, the savages have returned to these parts. I never thought I'd see the day. If it's my logs you need to slow these savages down, in my late wife Sarah's name, it's my logs you'll have. Now, what is your plan?"

Nathaniel quickly says to the French trader. "Jacques, to the river. Give us a crow's call when the canoes are precisely at the foot of the sluice. We'll need to release the logs at exactly the right time to do the most damage. We'll release the logs on your signal, and hopefully send the lot of them to a watery grave." "Oui, Oui, Nathaniel. Be waiting for my signal." Jacques replies as he quickly ambles down the steep riverbank.

As the canoes are entering the gorge where the log sluice lies, Chief Grey Lock suddenly orders the warriors to stop paddling. Chief Metallak looks at him and says, "Is something wrong? " Grey Lock answers, "Just an instinct telling me things aren't right here. It's probably nothing." Then he looks up to the top of the riverbank and spies Nathaniel watching from the trees. He quickly points Nathaniel out to Chief Metallak, "It's the English dog "Nathaniel" who escaped from our campsite! There could be more of the accursed English! Send twenty men to shore to climb that bank, and capture him now! He will not escape my wrath this time! The rest of you continue paddling down the river, if the fort know we're coming we must hurry to reach it before they are prepared for us."

Chief Metallak replies looking up at Nathaniel, "Consider it done Great Chief. Sokwaki warriors, take five of your canoes to shore and capture the Englishman!" The warriors reply, "Yes, Oh great chief, it will be done." as they furiously paddle their canoes to the shore. They beach the canoes in the sand and start running up the steep bank towards Nathaniel, giving out fierce war cries.

Nathaniel sees them coming and warns the others, "They're coming up the bank! Be ready men!" Nathaniel and the Farnsworths start firing down the bank to stop the warriors reaching the top. The warriors try to hide behind the trees on the bank, but the fire cuts them down. Grey

Lock witnesses this and shouts out, "Ambush! Ambush! Paddle fiercely now, or we'll be trapped in this ravine!

The flotilla starts to race down the river and as they reach the log sluice a cry rings out. "Caw! Caw!" Jacques gives his warning crow's call to the men above. Farnsworth's sons attempt to pull the pins on the log sluice, but they are wedged in too tightly. They watch as the first twenty canoes pass the log sluice harmlessly. Nathaniel quickly comes over to aid in releasing the mammoth logs. "Stand aside men!" He yells as he chops the sluices log pins into pieces with his ax. Without the supporting pins, the force of gravity takes over and the sluice is broken to pieces as the giant logs begin to roll and tumble down the steep bank.

An enormous rumble is heard in the ravine as Grey Lock looks up just in time to see that the flotilla will be crushed by the onslaught of the huge logs. He tries to warn the warriors shouting out, "To shore! To shore! Head to the far shore! Climb the far bank!" but it's too late, the logs are crashing violently into the flotilla before his warning cry is heard.

"Aieehh! Aieehh!" the warriors cry out as the logs crash into the fragile birch bark canoes that soon become smashed to pieces and are pulled under water in the river's strong undertow. Many warriors are trapped beneath the logs and the blue Connecticut River water turns red with Abenaki blood.

The river is now filled with a twenty-foot wide swath of logs that reaches both banks of the ravine and blocks the second half of the flotilla from passing. As the enormous force of the Connecticut's current pushes against the giant logs the water turns into a red colored rapid over the logjam.

The logjam has split the Abenaki flotilla in two, destroying at least twenty canoes in the center. The canoes upriver behind the logjam cannot pass because some of the logs have wedged themselves in the thick river bottom mud and hold the rest of the logs from floating downstream, blocking the river.

Some of the warriors in the surviving canoes climb onto the massive pile of logs and attempt to dislodge the logs stuck in the mud to allow them to move downstream with no avail. Many more warriors fall off of the logs and become trapped in the river's undertow. The surviving warriors climb back into their canoes and paddle to shore where they beach them and start running up the steep bank where the log sluice once was.

Jacques fires shots at the warriors as they come ashore and a few are killed, but the rest see him and return fire forcing him to retreat up the steep bank. As he reaches the top of the bank he exclaims to Nathaniel, "Run. Run now! The whole tribe is heading this way and we've no time!" He and Nathaniel mount their horses and start to leave the sluice site. Farnsworth and his sons stand motionless and Nathaniel shouts out, "On your horses now! The warriors will be upon us in no time." Farnsworth calmly replies, "We're staying put and will delay the tribe while you two escape. We're not leaving our homestead Indians or no. There are old mines in the hillside made by the early settlers that the natives haven't found yet. There we can escape them. Go now!"

Nathaniel replies, "Old mines? Where are these old mines?" Farnsworth answers, "Up that rocky hill behind the behind the sluice. We used the old mines when the Abenaki attacked us before the war. The old mines can only be reached by scaling a steep trail in the rocks, and the cliffs above them are forty feet tall and impassible by a man.

We've held out in the old mines many times, and no Abenaki's made it to them yet. We'll be safe there. This isn't my first Indian attack, and living in these parts, I don't think it will be the last. We were born here, and we'll die here if necessary. Ain't no red man forcing us off our land. In my late wife Sarah's name we're staying put."

Nathaniel looks up at the rocky hill smiling and replies, "This may just save our skins. We'll make our stand there." Farnsworth replies, "If we can reach the old mines and hold off the Indians until we block the entrance, we should be able to escape at the other end, a quarter mile upriver by Ashley's Ferry." "Well, it's a plan, and right now the best option we have. To the old mines!" Nathaniel shouts as he and Jacques jump off of their horses and start running towards the hill.

Suddenly twenty Sokwaki warriors reach the top of the river bank and begin firing at the settlers. One of Farnsworth's sons is surprised by the sudden attack and is shot in the back. He falls to the ground and is lying there motionless until Farnsworth quickly runs back, picks up his son's body with one arm and carries it across the clearing towards the hill, shouting out, "Follow me up the hill! We can pick these savages off as they reach the clearing and it'll take quite a bit of doing to dislodge us from there. I also have a surprise these savages won't be expecting."

The warriors run across the clearing firing their muskets while letting out piercing cries. Farnsworth leads the group up the hillside trail and they keep climbing until they finally find shelter in a shallow cave in the cliffs halfway to the old mine's entrance. Taking positions in the cave, they start firing at the warriors temporarily halting their advance to the edge of the clearing.

The five men hold off the attackers for a few minutes, but then are overrun as the warriors clamber up the hill and are about to reach the cave. The men are forced out of the cave and climb the rocky trail to the old mine entrance. They reach the entrance and are able to hold their position firing down the steep trail. The Indians attempt to follow, but are cut down by the settler's fire. Nathaniel and Jacques keep shooting down the hill while Farnsworth carries his wounded son to the old mine. Farnsworth's other son picks up his brother and they dive unseen into the hidden old mine, while Farnsworth shouts out to Nathaniel and Jacques, "C'mon now you two! We must go into the mine now!"

All of the men dive into the old mine except Farnsworth who stands at the old mine entrance digging through the rocks until he pulls out a black box with a plunger on top that is hitched to a wire leading down the hill.

"Now here's something they won't expect." He says as he pushes the plunger on the dynamite and dives into the mine. With a loud boom, the rocky hill turns into a landslide, sealing the hidden old mine's entrance with the settlers inside. The Abenaki try to retreat down the hill but are trapped beneath the tumbling rockslide.

Grey Lock and Metallak watch from the clearing as twenty or more warriors are buried in under the falling boulders. Grey Lock shouts out, "After them! Surround the hill and be sure no white man escapes." The Indians start trying to make their way up the hill, but now find it impassible with all of the fallen rocks. They go around the rockslide and reach the top of the hill forty feet above the old mine, but are unable to descend down the steep cliff. When they finally do reach the mine entrance, it has vanished with the settlers in the blasted rocks.

They search for the settlers for an hour until Grey Lock asks one of his warriors, "Where are the English? Where is "Nathaniel"? Did they escape?" The warrior answers, "I believe the English were crushed by their rock slide. We've seen no motion, nor heard any sound. All we can see is a pile of rocks."

Grey Lock speaks, "The river is blocked and the sun will be setting soon. Make camp here for the night. We must bury our dead and assess our losses. We attack with the rising sun. Collect the dead and prepare the ground for burials. Bring the damaged canoes ashore for repair. I know this will delay our arrival, but we have no choice. The element of surprise has been lost for now". Grey Lock then shouts out to the hills, "Nathaniel, I know you hear me. You will not escape me again, and soon you *will pay and* face my wrath!"

Chapter 13

The next morning everything seems quiet at the Fort at Number Four. Some of the children who are bored with being kept inside the fort go out into the courtyard and start playing stickball. The settler's wives start preparing breakfast, and the smell of bacon, eggs, and johnnycakes fills the air. The sleepy-eyed settlers get up and dress for the day, like the reality of their situation was just a bad nightmare given the calm of everyday life in this peaceful scene. The troops guarding the walls sleepily make their way to the Great Chamber for their morning breakfast.

Captain Stevens is awakened by the sounds of his dogs barking and growling out of the windows of his quarters. He looks at the dogs and says, "What's the matter boys, something amiss? Or are you still barking at those squirrels that were teasing you last night? Either way, I'd better go and see what you're fussing about." He rises, still in his uniform from the night before and slips on his boots.

His wife Elizabeth gets up and looks worriedly out the window at the tall grass of the Great Meadow and says, "Quite a lot of worry on your mind, eh Phineas? You didn't sleep well. Tossing and turning like the ocean all night, I'm surprised you found any sleep at all." Her husband answers, "Yes Elizabeth, quite a lot on all of our minds these days, matters being as they are. Now what are the dogs barking at? I'd best let them out anyways... C'mon boys." The captain opens the cabin door that leads to the stockade fenced in yard outside the clustered cabins and the dogs go running out. "Well, they're in a hurry about something, I'd better go have a look."

The dogs run though the grass and straight to the north wall of the fort and continue barking at the woods across the Great Meadow. Captain Stevens looks into the woods where the dogs are facing and notices movement in the trees. As he turns to return to his log cabin, he hears a loud thud in the area of the dogs. He turns back and sees a flaming arrow stuck into the stockade wall setting it on fire.

The outer wall of the fort was made of twelve-foot posts spaced four inches apart so no invaders could come through the walls but shots could be fired from within. He runs through his cabin to the inner courtyard of he fort and yells, "To Arms! To Arms! We are under attack! The north wall is on fire! Send buckets of water out through the trenches to the wall to put out the fire and be quick about it! This is not a drill!"

The troops hurriedly gobble up the last bites of their morning meal and come running into the courtyard. They quickly fill buckets of water from the well and race through the trenches to the outer courtyard where the stockade fence is on fire. As they do several more arrows hit the wall and the fire starts blazing brighter and soon a section of the wall ten feet wide is engulfed in flames.

Smoke pours out of the fifteen-foot tall stockade fence as the troops pour their buckets of water on it to douse the flames. Looking across he field in the direction of the incoming arrows they see nothing but a slight breeze rustling through the trees. The troops fire several musket rounds into the woods, but only silence follows.

As the fire is put out the Captain orders them back into the fort. Addressing the troops in the courtyard he says, "Men, we are under attack. Ten men fill all available buckets with water and bring them to the trenches now! Ten men to the trenches inside the walls to receive buckets of water in case they try to set the walls on fire again! Go now, and be quick about it!"

The troops bringing buckets of water to the trenches are met with musket and flaming arrow fire as they come out of the cabins and are forced back inside. The Indians attempt to push their advantage and start running across the field towards the fort but are cut down by the soldier's fire. Some flaming arrows do hit the wall but the troops in the trenches easily put them out. The shots fired at the fort are ineffectual as well, with most hitting the posts. The troop's fire does much more damage to the advancing Indians and they are forced to again retreat back into to the woods.

The guard in the watchtower shouts down to the Captain, "Captain Sir! You have to come up and look at this! I don't believe what I'm seeing!" Climbing the ladder into the watchtower Captain Stevens says, "Where Private? What do you see?" The Private replies, "There Captain, by the river landing. I first saw it before the battle began and thought it was a mass of logs floating down the river a mile away, but it's been moving so fast it has come a lot closer, I can now see it's something else. Take a look in my eyeglass sir, it's something like I've never seen before."

Looking into the eyeglass, Captain Stevens looks down to the river landing to see a dark mass coming to shore with great speed. Focusing the eyeglass in he sees that it is fifty or more large Abenaki canoes filled with brightly dressed, plumed-haired warriors. He shouts down to the courtyard. "I am seeing at least two hundred warriors at the river landing in war canoes! Lieutenant, quickly send twenty men out through the south gate and up the road by the river to fire upon them and delay their progress to the fort. Move now and be quick about it!"

The Captain shouts again. "Rangers take positions in the woods by the river landing. Fire on sight of any war canoes about to reach the landing. You two man the cannon! Fire two warning shots into the river north of the fort. We need to delay their reaching us and disorganize and confuse them any way we can."

As the cannon's warning shots are fired, two groups of Rangers ride out of the fort through the south gate. They are met almost immediately with the repeated fire of arrows and rifles as they attempt to cross the Great Clearing. They return fire upon the attackers, but their horses are cut down and they are left trying to take cover behind them, to shield themselves from the ever-increasing incoming fire. The Indians come out of the woods and again try to press their advantage.

Captain Stevens yells out "Retreat! Retreat!" and the remaining rangers race back into the fort. As the last of the men try to come through the south gate, they are hit by enemy fire. Soldiers firing out of the upstairs windows in the Great Chamber slow the Indian's advance while several of the other Rangers run out through the gate and retrieve their bodies.

Captain Stevens shouts out from the watchtower, "Fire the cannon over the south wall! All available men to the south gate! Shoot any enemy in sight and don't waste the gunpowder! Get the wounded into Dr. Hawkins' house and have him tend to their wounds! The battle's begun and we will need every able body we have." As he looks out from the watchtower he sees hundreds of brightly dressed Abenaki warriors now surrounding the fort on every side letting out deafening war cries a few feet from the walls.

He climbs down from the watchtower and addresses everyone inside, "Troops, settlers, we are surrounded on all sides by many Abenaki warriors with no way I can see to escape. The reinforcements I expected have not made it in time. As we hear their war cries and constant fire, we must be ready to expect the worst. Bring all of the women and children into the cabins and fortify the doors. We will protect you as long as we are able. If anyone has any prayers to say, I would say them now..."

Before the Captain can say any more, suddenly the Abenaki stop firing and move back to the edge of the woods. The Captain orders his men at the walls, "Hold your fire men! We'll need our ammunition for the enemy's return." Beating war drums replace the gunfire and screams that were heard over the battlefield as two brightly painted and feathered

Abenaki warriors on horseback cross the Great Meadow carrying a white flag of truce.

The sentry shouts out from the watchtower, "Captain, it's Chief Metallak, the one who was here before and it looks like another Abenaki with long grey hair and a grey face. He looks like a chief judging by his dress. They have stopped just outside the fort gate, and are motioning for someone to come out to talk to them."

The Captain climbs down from the tower and orders, "Open the gate! Killiam and Hastings come with me. We will go out and see what their demands are." The three men jump on their horses and rides out of the open gate to meet the two Abenaki chiefs. As the meet the two Chiefs, the Captain says to them, "Chief Metallak, I've told you my position on this and we will fight to the last man to keep our settlers safe. Attack if you will, but much Abenaki blood will be shed before the Fort at Number Four is taken."

Chief Metallak replies, "We have discussed this before Captain and I have tried to reason with you. But by Abenaki law this matter is now in the hands of Chief Grey Lock. It is his demands you will be hearing this day. You should heed his words."

Grey Lock speaks, "Kwai or hello Captain Stevens, I know your name through our legends. My name is Wawanolet, Chief Grey Lock and you should heed my words. I have no fear of any English retribution, nor do I place any faith in false English treaties. I have not come to the Connecticut River valley since the war against the English many years ago when many of your people were killed."

"We have your fort surrounded and you are now our prisoners. If I had my way we would kill you all here and now, but Chief Metallak has persuaded me to give you one last chance. You must surrender the Fort at Number Four immediately and gather your people and travel south to your

Fort Dummer in Brattleboro never to return. All of the English in this river valley north of Fort Dummer must do the same. We are reclaiming this land for the Abenaki people, and you are not welcome here."

" I see that you have gathered your people inside the fort's walls for protection. However, by doing so you have left the settlement vacant and open to attack. If you do not agree to our terms, we will burn the town of Charlestown house by house while you watch helplessly through those walls unable to escape."

"We are in no hurry on this matter, nor are we starving or lacking in supplies as we were in 1747. We have you surrounded and will wait until your stores run out, and this time you will come crawling to us for food and supplies."

"I will give you two of your hours to consider this and after that will burn one house every hour until the town of Charlestown is a pile of burning embers. Consider this well, Captain. If you wish to surrender, lead your troops out of these fort walls and we will consider sparing them, and allow them to gather their belongings to move south to your Fort Dummer. I will await your reply."

Chapter 14

A few hours earlier, Ethan Allen and a hundred Green Mountain Boys are crossing the Connecticut River at Ashley's Ferry a few miles north of the fort. Nathaniel, Jacques and the Farnsworths ride up on horseback to meet Ethan and David Farnsworth as they ride off the ferry.

David is surprised to see them and noticing the blood coming from his father's arm he says, "Father, you've been shot. Are you alright?" His father answers, "Just a flesh wound son, I'll be ok." David replies, "Have you been attacked? I was sent by Captain Stevens to Bennington to enlist the Green Mountain Boys aid against a surprise attack by the Abenaki tribe. We left will arrive in time."

Nathaniel answers, "We hope you are in time as well. The Abenaki were planning to attack yesterday, but we were able to slow them down a bit with the aid of your Father's log sluice. He was wounded in the battle. We dropped the logs on the Abenakis paddling down the river. They suffered many casualties and were forced to halt their attack for the night. They spent the night at the log sluice, but I imagine they must be attacking the fort as we speak."

Nathaniel walks over to Ethan, shakes his hand and asks, "Be ye Ethan Allen? I am Nathaniel Jarvis, a settler here in the valley. My homestead's already been attacked by the Abenaki, and we are heavily outnumbered. Have our prayers been answered with the reinforcements of the Green Mountain Boys?"

Ethan answers, "Yes, I am Ethan Allen of the Green Mountain Boys. Your David Farnsworth alerted us of the situation with the Abenaki. We came as fast as we were able and I hope we've arrived in time. What has occurred?"

Nathaniel explains to Ethan, "First without provocation, my homestead was burned to the ground by Grey Lock and the Missisquoi warriors in a surprise attack. Then we discovered the warriors were on their way to attack the Fort at Number Four. We created a diversion to delay Grey Lock and the Abenaki warriors from reaching the fort which stopped them yesterday We let loose around fifty giant pines from the top of Mr. Farnsworth's log sluice a quarter of a mile down the river from here and hit the Abenaki canoes that were passing in the river below. Many warriors were killed, and Mr. Farnsworth here blasted some dynamite after that, that killed even more. We destroyed some but I believe the rest are on their way to the fort as I speak."

"We escaped into an old mine in the hillside, but were trapped there by the rock slide until we were able to make our way out. I would estimate we killed at least seventy warriors. I don't know any more as we were trapped inside until this morning when we dug our way out at the other end."

Allen says, "You came up with an ingenuous plan. You used the resources available to you so the few could stop the many. It's reminiscent of Captain Stevens' famous siege." Nathaniel answers, "Well, actually Captain Stevens came up with the plan, we just carried it out." Ethan chuckles and replies, "So the old man still has some tricks up his sleeve, very admirable. I hope it's not too late to save the fort. Grey Lock you say. I didn't think that murderer was still alive. He's killed many a settler with his surprise attacks. If the battle at the fort's begun we cannot delay in leaving."

"Agreed" says Nathaniel, "We must not lose a minute. I've seen the Abenaki warriors numbers and even though we killed some of them, there must still be well over four hundred warriors." Ethan replies, "We'll even that up a bit, I've brought a hundred men. However, we must attempt to keep our presence a secret. I imagine the Abenaki are well entrenched around the fort and a frontal assault could be disastrous."

Ethan replies, "Yes, we'll need every advantage we can get. We're still outnumbered but we will use Grey Lock's own surprise tactics against him. When we arrive at the fort we must survey the enemy's position and find any weaknesses in it to create our own advantages. Time is of the essence."

Ethan then commands his men, " On to the fort! We must remain as silent as possible so the enemy doesn't hear us coming. Nathaniel, you know this trail. Let us know when we are nearing the fort and we will regroup and make our plans then." Nathaniel responds as he climbs on his horse, "I'll lead the way. Follow me. Mr. Farnsworth, you and your boys better stay home and tend to your wounds. Thank you for all of your help."

As Nathaniel leads them down the river trail they come to a clearing overlooking the Town of Charlestown. As they look down into the town they see clouds of smoke rising above the town. Nathaniel says, "That smoke looks like it's rising from about where the Fort at Number Four lies. There must be a battle raging. We must quicken our pace to arrive in time. Hahh!" He shouts at his horse as he and the troops start racing down the hill and into Charlestown.

As the group nears the fort they hear the sound of gunfire that suddenly stops. Ethan orders the troops to halt and remain quiet and says, "What has happened? Why has the battle ceased? I don't believe that Captain Stevens would give up the fort so easily. Let us move in closer to have a better view."

As they move in closer to the north side of the fort they watch as Captain Stevens and his escort ride out of the fort gate and start crossing the Great Meadow. Two Abenaki chiefs carrying a white flag ride out to meet them.

Nathaniel says, "Ethan, that's Chief Grey Lock, the one who destroyed my homestead. Has Captain Stevens lost his nerve? It appears that Stevens is surrendering to him, but why the battle's just begun? What are our choices here? We are a hundred strong, but have we arrived too late?" Jacques intervenes, "I don't believe old Phineas would give up the entire Connecticut River valley without a fight. He's a feisty old man, he must have something up his sleeve."

Ethan responds, "Trick or no, what we are seeing could mean the end of the Fort at Number Four, the English settlements, our land grants, and the beginning of a reign of terror up and down the Connecticut River valley. We must let Stevens know we are here and not to surrender the fort quite yet. But how?" Nathaniel thinks for a moment and then says to Ethan, "We must fire all of our muskets at once and then charge their position. It will alert Captain Stevens that help has arrived, and surprise the Abenaki as well."

Ethan answers incredulously, "Fire our muskets and give away our position? I highly doubt that that will help the situation. We should remain quiet, and see what transpires when Stevens reaches the Abenaki position. He may have a plan as well. Hold your fire men."

They continue watching Stevens and his party cross the field and meet with the Abenaki party. The two leaders talk for a few minutes and then the Captain returns to the fort. Ethan says indignantly, "I've seen enough. We must surprise them now before it's too late. We will try Nathaniel's plan. Fire all of your muskets into the air at once and prepare to charge the Abenaki positions. This battle's not over yet, in fact it's just begun. Are you ready men? Load your flintlocks now and prepare to fire on my command." The troops load their muskets with powder and shot and raise them into the air. Ethan commands, "Ready... Aim... Fire!"

The men fire their muskets in unison in to the air and the sound of a hundred muskets firing at once thunders across the hills. Ethan orders his men to reload their muskets and charge the Abenaki ranks, and the

Green Mountain boys ride out of the woods into the Great Clearing. The sound alerts the Abenaki warriors who start moving towards the Green Mountain Boys' position on the north side of the fort from all directions. It also surprises Captain Stevens and Grey Lock, who turn in the Green Mountain Boys direction to see what the commotion is about only to see a hundred men riding in their direction.

Grey Lock says to Captain Stevens, "A trick? You will die for this Englishman. I will take your life here and now myself." Before Grey Lock is able to raise his musket to fire, Private Killiam fires at Grey Lock and hits his horse knocking the horse and Grey Lock to the ground. Seeing their leader being fired upon the Abenaki come out of the woods and fire at Captain Steven's party. Stevens sheaths his sword and starts to ride back to the fort, but his horse is hit by musket fire and he too falls to the ground.

The Green Mountain Boys start their charge from the north across the Great Meadow and break through the Abanaki's ranks and are about to reach the south side of the fort outside the gate where the leaders are meeting. Seeing them, Grey Lock retreats towards the woods leaving his horse lying in the field. Chief Metallak takes command ordering the warriors surrounding the fort to charge the Green Mountain Boys with all of their force.

Captain Stevens and his men are caught in the crossfire of the attack. As Stevens tries to climb on Corporal Hawkins' horse to return to the fort, Metallak fires at Hawkins hitting the Corporal in the chest and knocking him to the ground. Private Killiam quickly rides over to help them, but his horse is shot as well and the horse falls to the ground trapping Killiam underneath. Stevens pulls Killiam from underneath his fallen horse and helps him to his feet. They then try to get Hawkins up, but his wounds are too severe.

"John, c'mon now get up! We've no time to dally here."
Killiam urges his fellow soldier. Hawkins answers gasping, "It's too late for me. Save yourselves." The Captain bends down and says to him, "Let's go Charles! That's an order!"

Hawkins answers, "You were right about an attack, sir. I just didn't know I would be on the receiving end... It was action I wanted, and action I found... I will die a happy soldier now... Please leave me and save yourselves." The Captain answers, "You're a brave soldier John, I will see to it that you haven't fallen in vane, now on your feet man." Hastings tries to get up but is unable to.

Nathaniel reaches Captain Stevens and his party and shouts out, "Phineas jump on my horse!" Captain Stevens answers, "I'm not leaving my men here in the field. Take Corporal Hawkins, he's been wounded." Stevens lifts Hawkins limp body on to Nathaniel's horse who carries them back inside the fort gate. Ethan and Jacques arrive picking up Captain Stevens and Private Killiam on their horses and bringing them back to the safety of the fort as well.

Once inside the fort Private Killiam carries Corporal Hawkins in to Doctor Hastings' house. He puts him on the doctors' table and says to the doctor, "He's been hit pretty bad Doc, is there anything you can do for him?" The Doctor replies, "It's a chest wound, those are usually the most fatal. Let me take a look."

The Doctor pulls out his stethoscope and places it on Hastings chest. He says, "He's hardly breathing, but there is a chance. We'll have to operate right now to remove that musket ball. Hand me some of those towels to stop the blood." Motioning to a table beside Killiam. The Doctor takes the towels and cleans up the blood coming from Hastings chest, and orders Killiam, "Get me that bottle of Whiskey over on the cabinet. It'll clean up the wound and anesthetize him enough so we can remove the shell."

Meanwhile, the Abenaki charge is about to reach the fort's south walls when the Green Mountain Boys' fire forces them to retreat back to the tree line. The Abenaki warriors to the east and west sides of the fort advance and the Green Mountain Boys find themselves surrounded on three sides and are forced to retreat towards the fort. They battle fiercely against the onslaught, but are pushed back to into the fort's south gate.

Once inside the already crowded fort, the Green Mountain Boys dismount and fifty men clamber to the roof of the Great Chamber to help the trooper return the enemy fire. From the safety of the roof they are able to easily pick off the Abenaki warriors as they advance on the south side. The Abenaki are forced back to the woods to regroup for another attack.

Once the attacking fire ceases the men on the roof climb down into the courtyard, and Captain Stevens quickly walks over to Ethan and shakes his hand saying, "Good to see you again Ethan, it's been years... Thank the Lord you and your men arrived just in the nick of time. You saved our lives and you have my gratitude. Now we must make plans to drive these invaders back from whence they came. Come into my office and we'll discuss this."

"Ethan answers, "It's good to see you again as well Phineas. The years have passed since we first met. When we heard of your predicament, we came as quickly as we could. We must devise some plan of action. Show me your office." He and the Captain walk into the Captain's office and close the door.

Grey Lock and Metallak are meeting in the Abenaki campsite to plan a new attack when Metallak says, "I did not expect the arrival of the famed Ethan Allen and the Green Mountain Boys. We outnumber the English troops by a much smaller margin now. How shall we proceed now Grey Lock?"

Grey Lock answers, "No, I never anticipated their reinforcements either, but for now we pushed them back into the fort. This leaves us a few options. We could start burning down houses in the town of Charlestown as we promised. This would draw the troops out of the fort and we could be ready for them and shoot them as they come out of the fort gate. On the other hand, we could directly attack the fort and burn the fort walls trapping them inside. Either method would be effective, what say ye Metallak?"

Metallak replies, "I would say that both plans have merit, but burning the town would draw them out of the fort and leave them and the fort open for a direct attack. I move that we loot and pillage the vacant town, forcing the English out of the fort and then we move in and lay siege to the fort.

Grey Lock replies, " I would say that we have enough men to start both plans simultaneously. We can create a diversion on the far side of the fort to take their attention away from the town, while at the same time begin burning the vacant town." He orders his warriors, "Burn the fort wall! Start on the far side and light a fire that will engulf the entire fort in flames. Go now!"

Captain Stevens and Ethan Allen are meeting at the same time to plan their own strategy. Stevens says, "We are trapped inside the fort with a large attacking force just outside the gate. We must somehow send troops to defend the empty town of Charlestown or the Abenaki will destroy the town, pillaging and taking what they will."

Ethan replies, "Yes, we are trapped similar to sheep in a pen, we must make a move or the Abenaki will starve us out or worse. I believe we should send a force out through the main gate that can hold back or delay the Abenaki from burning the town. As the front gate is the only entrance to the fort, I don't think we have much choice."

Stevens replies, "I concur. Though the Abenaki still outnumber us by a sizeable margin, we still have two factors in our favor. One, as they arrived in canoes, most of the Abenaki are on foot. They have only a limited number of horses whereas we have a troop of Rangers with horses here at the fort and a hundred Green Mountain Boys on horseback as well. Two, we have several cannon in the fort, and they have only muskets. If we fire several cannon shots at their ranks on the road to Charlestown, it should break their ranks enough so a force on horseback could break through and take up a position in town."

Ethan answers as he gets up to leave, "Yes, that is a good plan Captain. We will choose our swiftest riders for the mission. I suggest we send a combination of my Green Mountain Boys and your Rangers. That way we will have fresh troops as well as men who know the area and town who can choose the best spot to hold off the attackers. I will go now and search my ranks for the best choices."

The Captain answers, "It's settled then. I will do the same and search my ranks for the best choices as well. I will also alert the cannoneers of our plan, and they will be ready to fire upon our command. We will meet back here in an hour and put our plan into action." "Agreed." Answers Ethan shaking the Captains hand and walking out of the office.

The Captain says to the guard stationed outside the door, "Send for David Farnsworth and Private Killiam. Tell them to come to my office immediately. It is a matter of most importance." The guard leaves his post and goes off to complete his mission.

Simon Sartwell and Josiah Hubbard are walking through the fort's courtyard. Simon says to Josiah, "Well Josiah, you were opposed to maintaining the fort and look what's happened. Without the fort and all of these Indians attacking, we'd surely be goners by now."

Josiah answers, "Yes, saved, but for what? Those savages have probably already ransacked the town and taken any valuables we may have. Why isn't Captain Stevens doing something about saving our town? God knows it'll probably be a burnt wasteland by the time we return. He has plenty of men now, he should be doing something."

Simon rebukes, "For someone who's opposed Captain Stevens for quite some time, now you're the one second guessing his strategies? Why don't you fall into line? Captain Stevens and the fort are the only reasons there still is a settlement here and we can thank him for all of our lives."

Josiah replies, "I'll remember that when Grey Lock is burning this fort and we are all trapped inside. I'd better see some sign of action from the old Captain, or as a selectman I will take action myself. Good day to you sir, and I hope we live long enough to meet again." The two men part ways and storm off towards their lean-tos.

As the two men are about to enter their lean-tos, a fire breaks out on the fort's north wall. Captain Stevens orders his men, "Send men with buckets of water to the outer perimeter inside the north fort wall! First, douse those flames and then start firing for all you're worth! We'll start a bucket brigade from the well and pass out enough buckets of water to put out any new fires."

The men start running out through the trenches from the log cabins into the outer perimeter of the fort carrying buckets, but most are cut down by enemy fire. The Captain orders out, "Fire several cannon shots over the north wall!" The Rangers aim the cannon and the blasts land in the field outside the fort wall and force the Abenaki to retreat back towards the woods, enabling the troops to reach the fort's north wall and start putting out the flames. Then as it was in the Siege of 1747, the troops soon are passing enough water out to douse the flames and the fire on the north wall is extinguished.

Watching from windows in the lean-tos, Simon says to Josiah, "A plan of action you wanted, and action you've received. Stevens saved the fort in '47 and he's saving us now. Enough of your belly aching man, let's help the troops instead of bickering. We must support Captain Stevens, especially at a time like this."

Josiah answers as he watches the flames being put out, "The old man still has his wits about him, that's for sure, but I still don't see a way to save our homes." Simon answers, "You'll never change Josiah, and sometimes you can't see the forest for the trees. I'm just thankful that Stevens is in charge and not a naysayer such as yourself." Simon walks out of the lean-to and starts helping the men passing water out through the trenches.

Grey Lock says to Metallak, "The diversion is complete and now we will burn their town. Send the warriors from the north side of the fort to the road into the settlement and order them to start burning the houses down one by one." The Abenaki warriors begin racing towards the town with many war cries, but as they do cannon fire from the fort begins to land on the road and many of the warriors are cut down.

Almost simultaneously, the Green Mountain Boys and Steven's Rangers on horseback led by Ethan Allen, David Farnsworth, and Private Killiam come out of the fort gate and ride towards the remaining Abenaki force. The Abenaki warriors on foot are no match for the riders and many enemy warriors are shot as they attempt to escape the gunfire.

As the troops reach the town, Farnsworth guides them to the Town Hall. The Town Hall is a solid brick building that sits on top of a steep rise overlooking the town in all directions, the perfect spot for a few men to hold off any attackers. Ethan orders the men to take a position in the second floor of the town hall and prepare for any enemy advance. The troops take their positions in the windows on all four sides of the building and take aim peering down the steep bank.

The Abenaki advance to the foot of the rise and begin firing at the building with little results as the defenders quickly shoot down any attempt made to climb the hill. Grey Lock sees this and orders his men to leave a residual force at the town hall and to begin burning houses in the village one at a time.

By chance the Abenaki warriors choose Josiah Hubbard's house to burn first. As they throw their lit torches through the wooden house's windows, the building is quickly engulfed in flames. The sentry in the watchtower sees this and reports to the captain, "Sir, the warriors are burning the houses! I believe Mr. Hubbard's house has already been destroyed by fire. Shall we send out more men to protect the town, sir?" The Captain replies, "We must maintain the fort at all costs. We can't afford to lose any more men by sending them into the village. We'll have to hope that the troops in town will be able to deal with the fires."

Simon Hartwell hears this while he's passing buckets of water to the troops and says to Josiah, "A bit of irony, eh Josiah? I guess you won't have to worry about giving your farm away now. The native tribe has moved in and if we do make it out of this you *will* be living under a tree. Ahh, for the good old days, when all we had to worry about was the monthly drills... I guess we've learned that maintaining a fort on the western frontier is not an option, given the recent events."

Josiah shouts out with dismay, "What! My house is on fire!" He climbs up into the watchtower and sees his house in flames, and yells down to the Captain, "Captain Stevens, I demand that you send more troops into town before the entire village is destroyed. I'm a Selectman! You work for the town!"

The Captain looks up at Josiah and says, "But Mr. Hubbard, as you said before there is no reason for this quote "waste of time and effort called the troop stationed at the Fort at Number 4" unquote. If I could, I would send more men in to save the settlement, but as for now, we will maintain our position here... We can take this up at the next Selectman's meeting if any of us are still alive..."

Josiah climbs down from the watchtower enraged and storms towards his lean-to shouting, "Stevens, you'll pay for this! I've a mind to..." But as he's about to finish his statement, Simon walks over and pours a bucket of water over his head saying, "Now, you'll calm down. Lead, follow, or get out of the way." Everyone inside the fort starts laughing as Josiah stomps off into his lean-to.

The Captain orders out, "Silence all of you! We've no time for idle chat! The entire valley is counting on our actions here today. Nathaniel and Jacques come into my office. If anyone else has any questions about my actions they can see me there." The three men walk into the Captain's office closing the door.

Chapter 15

As the Abenaki forces are focused on the town hall, a lone English rider races in from the east. Unnoticed by the attackers, he makes his way to the fort gate and shouts out to the watchtower, "I bring urgent news from Governor Benning Wentworth! I must speak with Captain Stevens at once!" Recognizing the rider to be the messenger sent to the Governor's mansion in Portsmouth the sentry orders the gate to be open.

Once inside the exhausted rider almost falls off of his horse, but stays on his feet and stumbles to Captain Steven's office where he collapses on the steps. Hearing this, Nathaniel runs out of the office and helps the man to his feet, giving him a drink of water from his canteen and says, "What word bring you from the Governor? Has he accepted my proposal of giving the Abenaki territory west of the Connecticut?"

The messenger reaches into his coat and pulls out the proclamation signed by Governor Wentworth as Nathaniel helps him to his feet and into the office where Captain Stevens is sitting behind his desk. He places the parcel on Captain Stevens' desk and says, "He granted your request, sir. If the Abenaki remove their forces to the west bank of the Connecticut and cease all hostilities, they will be granted a sizeable portion of unclaimed land between the Connecticut and Hudson Rivers where they can continue their way of life unhindered by the English in the surrounding territories. I've ridden a fortnight without stopping to bring you this message, but am I too late? I see the fort is surrounded. Have I arrived in time?"

The Captain begins reading the document bearing Governor Wentworth's official seal and says to Nathaniel, "Truly, the eyes of all people are upon us. I would never have thought that the Royal Governor would give in to your preposterous plan... But he did, and there is his Royal Seal. Now, as a sworn subject of King George, who Governor Benning Wentworth is a loyal servant, I must carry out this proclamation."

"But how? Grey Lock and Metallak have us at a severe disadvantage. Our men in the town hall cannot hold out forever against such tremendous numbers, nor can we here hold the fort for long even with our reinforcements."

He orders the sentry at the door, " Tell the sentry in the watchtower to lower the Red Ensign and raise a white flag of surrender. This will hopefully create a temporary ceasefire where we can present this plan to the Abanaki chiefs. Tell all men to cease fire and send word to the Abenaki that we will meet the chiefs outside the fort's gate."

The sentry leaves to complete his tasks and Nathaniel excitedly says to the Captain, "This could mean the dawning of a new day on the British Empire. If the Governor is giving in to the Abenaki demands, possibly he will hear the cries of the colonists about his unfair practices. Though we are considered British subjects, we colonists are scraping for our own survival in the untamed wilderness of the new World while trying to abide by the King's unfair laws. There's a rising tide of rebellion throughout the colonies. Maybe now the King will listen to his own colonist's demands."

The Captain answers, "I cannot believe that Governor Wentworth has actually granted a sizeable piece of land to the native people, especially for no profit. Rumor has had it over the last few years that the Governor has been granting land he didn't actually have rights over to line his own pockets, and there's also been talk of corruption in his administration. I imagine he must be concerned about the Abenaki rising. If this fort falls and the Abenaki regain their land, he would lose his claim over all of his land grants west of the Connecticut, and many to the east of the river as well."

"If this document didn't bear his official seal, I would not consider it to be legitimate. It does, however, and thusly I must act accordingly. I will prepare to meet the Abenaki chiefs and present them with Governor Wentworth's offer."

Nathaniel quickly responds, "Let me go with you Captain. I've discussed this very proposal with Chief Grey Lock when he held me prisoner. He seemed to be acceptable of a solution that would let his people return to their former way of life without English intervention. I think I can help lead Grey Lock to accept my solution, as the Governor has, and we can end this bloodshed."

The Captain looks over at Nathaniel, and then at the flag of surrender being raised in the watchtower and says, "Saddle your horse Nathaniel, we'll be leaving shortly. After all of these years of maintaining the peace here against any possible intrusion, I wouldn't have believed that the flag of surrender would go up over my fort. I've spent years and years keeping the fort and the citizens of Charlestown prepared for the eventuality of an attack from either the Indians or the French. My troops and I would lay down our lives for this western post.

He places his hand on Nathaniel's shoulder and adds, "We must see to it that the Abenaki accept your plan, Nathaniel. Our very lives are depending on it. If you have some knowledge of Chief Grey Lock, we must use it and every advantage we can muster to help all of us out of this situation. In fewer words, this may be our last chance: Failure is not an option. Saddle your horse, and we'll meet at the fort gate."

Grey Lock and Metallak watch as the Red Ensign flag is lowered and the white flag of surrender is raised in the watchtower. Metallak says to Grey Lock, "Does this mean that Stevens is surrendering? We can save many of our people's lives if the battle is finished now." Grey Lock answers, "It could be another English trick. They could be attempting to bring us out in the open for another surprise attack. We lost quite a few warriors during their last ruse."

Then Grey Lock sees Captain Stevens and Nathaniel coming through of the fort gate unarmed and carrying the white flag of surrender. He says, "Stevens is bringing Nathaniel out with him. Nathaniel will not escape my wrath this time. Join me Metallak, and we will ride out and see what trickery the English dog Nathaniel has in mind this time. Order the warriors to take aim at both men and be ready to fire on my command." The warriors line up behind the tall pines at the edge of the Great Meadow as both parties ride out to meet.

Grey Lock speaks first, "What is your offer Englishman. We grow tired of your trickery. Are you ready to surrender the fort and our stolen territories or will we finish you now? Answer quickly, my patience with you is wearing thin."

Captain Stevens speaks holding out the Governor's Royal decree, "Chief Grey Lock and Chief Metallak, I bring word from the Royal Governor of a solution to both of our situations. He pauses seeing the warriors lined up behind the trees and taking aim. "This is no trick and I carry a signed and sealed document from Royal Governor Benning Wentworth. This document offers the Abenaki people a chance to continue to thrive as they did before the English arrival on these shores. It offers your tribes a portion of land between the Connecticut and Hudson Rivers where they can live as they always have without our intervention."

Grey Lock replies, "Another worthless paper? I don't think we will be fooled by another one of the English's lies. If that is all you have to offer, you'd have done better to stay inside the safety of your fort's walls. Warriors take aim!" He says raising his hand signaling the warriors to prepare to fire.

Nathaniel answers, "Oh Great Chief Grey Lock, remember when I was your captive and we spoke about a solution that would benefit both of our peoples? I sent the solution we discussed to the Governor and he has approved it with the English King's Royal Seal... Wawanolet, I appeal to you in the name of many of both our people's lives. At least let me read the Royal Governor's decree to you before you make your decision."

Metallak intervenes, "I can read the White Man's markings as I learned from reading many of your worthless treaties. I have also seen the Governor's Royal Seal before on many of your papers. Give me that paper and I will judge if it has any value."

The Captain hands the document to Chief Metallak. He starts reading it, then puts it down to confer with Grey Lock, and says, "The English are offering to let us retain a large portion of our former lands if we desist in our mission and move to the west bank of the Connecticut River. I recognize the Governor's Royal Seal as authentic... Grey Lock, this appears to be a valid land grant."

Grey Lock takes the piece of paper and stares at it saying, "We have seen enough of the White Man's lies. How do I know this is true? I have been warring many seasons with the English. This is probably another trick." Captain Stevens says to the Abenaki chiefs, "Chief Metallak, have I ever lied to you? You know my words to be true after our years of dealings at my trading post. "

Metallak answers, "No Captain Stevens, in all of my years of trading with you, you have never lied to me. Since you were our captive many years ago, my people have always honored your word, as you have honored ours. Grey Lock, this could be the end of our people's woes. If Captain Stevens honors this new treaty, I would honor it as well."

Nathaniel speaks, "Grey Lock, this is the very plan we discussed back at my homestead, and now my words have come true. If you agree to accept the unclaimed lands between the two rivers as a homeland for your people, the days of warring with the White Man will end. The Abenaki will own a portion of the Dawnlands to do with as they will. What say you?"

Grey Lock replies, "Your foolish English belief that people "own" the sacred ground is very foreign and strange to the Abenaki beliefs. We do not trample the earth and fill it with permanent dwellings and unmoving farmlands that spoil the ground underneath as you do. Since the dawn of time the Abenaki have treasured the Dawnlands and since the English arrival on our shores, we see nothing but destruction to Ndakinna. If there is land where my people can live freely, and we can save even a part of Ndakinna from your intrusion, I must consider this seriously."

Chief Grey Lock orders the warriors to drop their arms and says to Captain Stevens while handing him the land grant, "We must have a tribal meeting to discuss this. We will cease hostilities in the meantime and for now we will consider this a truce until the morning. What say ye?"

Captain Stevens answers, " I will agree to a truce, and I am willing to give you enough time to consider the Governor's offer. We will meet back here tomorrow when the sun reaches its peak in the sky. Consider well Great Chiefs, the destiny of both our peoples is depending on your decision."

Both parties return back across the Great Meadow and the sentry opens the fort gate and lets Captain Stevens and Nathaniel into the fort. Jacques runs over to meet them and find out what happened at the meeting. Jacques asks Captain Stevens, "How did the meeting go? Will the Abenaki accept Governor Wentworth's proposal?"

The Captain answers, "They are considering it. I gave then a day to discuss it. We'll know tomorrow when we meet again. I am hopeful, but not sure what their decision will be. For now, all we can do is wait. Private Killiam, order the men to maintain lookout posts on rotation and for the rest to return to their quarters for rest."

Jacques replies, "At least now we have a chance. If they accept

Nathaniel's proposal, peace will return to the valley, and we can all return to our lives. Your proposal has merit Nathaniel, I hope the Abenaki see its worth." Nathaniel adds, "I hope the British keep their end of the bargain. I have seen Wentworth's grants before, and some aren't worth the paper they're written on. We can all pray they do."

Captain Stevens says, "For now we have a temporary ceasefire. I hope Ethan and the men in the town hall are alright. I haven't heard any gunfire from town recently. Let us hope they've survived this ordeal. As for the Green Mountain Boys still here in the fort, you can find food and shelter in the Great Chamber. I thank you all for volunteering to come to our aid, and we will provide food and rest for you there." With that the men go off to their quarters for some well-deserved rest.

Chapter 16

At the Abenaki campsite in a grove of giant White Pine trees across the Great Meadow from the fort, the tribal council is considering Governor Wentworth's proposal. Chief Metallak speaks first, "I was sent here from the Sokwaki and Cowass councils to seek a path to peace with the English. This proposal offers this. I move that we accept the English Governor's proposal and take his land grant so we can return to our sacred traditions. My vote, and the votes of the two combined tribes, is yes."

Chief Grey Lock replies, "We have seen many treaties and offers from the English which have all turned out to be false or lies. How do we know that this is not another one? We must consider Abanaki values before we enter into any agreement with the English. How do we know that this offer is a true one after the White Man's history of lies?"

A Sokwaki warrior speaks, "Oh Great Chiefs, tradition tells us that we must consider the Three Truths before making a decision of this size. I move that the tribal council vote on this now. My wife and family at home and all of the Abenaki families would suffer if we make the wrong decision without considering the Three Truths first." Chief Metallak agrees saying, "Yes, any decision by the Abenaki council must consider our most sacred beliefs. Do you agree to abide by the council's decision, Chief Grey Lock?" Grey Lock replies, "Whatever my personal thoughts are on this matter, yes, I will follow whatever decision the tribal council makes."

Chief Metallak answers, "It is settled then. We will have each of the three tribes choose three delegates to the voting council. Missisquoi, Cowass, and Sokwaki tribes vote now to choose your delegates." The three tribes confer and choose three delegates each who are sent to Chiefs Metallak and Grey Lock who complete the tribal council.

Chief Metallak speaks, "Delegates, the decision we make today will determine the future of our peoples for many generations to come. Do not make your judgments lightly. We must consider each of the Three Truths and a majority vote will our actions on this matter."

Chief Grey Lock speaks, "Missisquoi warriors, we have traveled far to complete our mission of saving our sacred lands. While we've been gone from our homes, hunting, fishing, and crops have become neglected. Though we must return to our homes to tend to these things, we must return with a decision that benefits all of our people. I feel that the English offer could be false. They have lied to and cheated us many times before. Consider this when making your choice whether to accept or decline this proposal."

Chief Metallak speaks, "The words that Chief Grey Lock speak are true. The English have not been reliable in their previous agreements with the Abenaki people. We have been pushed ever further off of our lands and their foreign diseases have ravaged our tribes as well. However, today's vote could determine whether we exist as a people at all. The lands the English are offering us hold no great value to them."

"They do not hold the same values as our people of hunting, fishing, and keeping the Dawnlands a sacred place. The map sent to us showed the hilly terrain we are being offered. It holds no value to them, as it is mostly hilltops and mountain ranges. But for our people, it would mean regaining some of our previous lands where we could live in peace. My vote will be to accept the proposal and return to our sacred beliefs. Consider this well my brothers, and let the voting begin."

Chief Grey Lock addresses the Tribal Delegates, "Peace: Is it preserved? What say the council on the First Truth?" A Sokwaki warrior rises and says, "How can peace be preserved when we are already at war? I would vote for any chance at returning to peace and our homelands even if there is doubt that the English offer could be false."

A Missisquoi warrior rises and responds, "We have traveled from our home land at the far end of our sacred lake Bitawbagw, the lake the English call Champlain. Since Odzihozo created the river valleys and lakes by dragging himself about with his hands, the Abenaki people have held Lake Bitawbagw as their sacred homeland. Offering our people a region that is mostly mountaintops would not satisfy the Missisquoi. I vote we try to make a better agreement with the English and receive a fair amount of ndakinna, our land."

Chief Metallak speaks, "We will put this to a silent vote. I will pass around this clay pot. If you believe out first truth is upheld by accepting the English proposal, make two marks on a piece of bark and place it in the pot. If you are opposed, make one mark on a piece of bark. Peace: Is it preserved? Vote now."

The clay pot is passed around and the council members each place their piece of bark in the clay pot. Both chiefs count the votes and Chief Metallak announces the decision. "The First Truth is upheld by a vote of seven to four. We must consider the other truths now. Righteousness: Is it moral?"

Grey Lock speaks out, "I can't see how any agreement with the English dogs can be moral. In my opinion, we should drive these invaders back into the sea. I don't see how this proposal can pass our second Truth."

Metallak answers, "We cannot hold ourselves responsible for other nations actions. The morality spoken of in this truth means maintaining the righteousness of our people. Under these grounds I would say this agreement passes the Second Truth."

Grey Lock becomes enraged and says, "You are attempting to bypass our sacred laws in order to have peace with the White Men. I say we put this to a vote here and now and forego any more discussion."

They pass the clay pot around once again and the vote is ten to one in favor passing the Second Truth.

Grey Lock rises insulted and says, "My opinion does not seem to matter with this council. I will leave you now to make the decision. Under our laws I will abide by the decision the tribal council makes." He gets up and storms out of the council meeting.

Metallak goes on, trying to keep the meeting together and says, "Regardless of Grey Lock's opinion on this matter, the council must come to a decision today with or without him. We shall continue. The Third Truth, Power: Does it preserve the integrity of the group? I have no doubt that the Governor's proposal passes the third test. Let us put it to a vote now." He passes the clay pot a third time and receives a unanimous decision in favor of the Third Truth.

Metallak rises and says, "The Tribal Council has spoken. We will agree to the English Governor's proposal. I will alert Captain Stevens of our decision. Warriors, prepare to break camp and return to our new homelands. Our mission here is done." The Tribal Delegates rise and return to their campsites to tell the warriors of the Tribal decision.

Metallak walks over to the Missisquoi campsite and finds Grey Lock still fuming about the Tribal Council's decision while the Missisquoi warriors are hastily breaking down their campsite. Metallak says to him, "Oh Great Chief Grey lock, we've completed our mission here, it's time to return to our new homeland, old friend."

Grey Lock throws his musket to the ground and says grudgingly, "A treaty? ... With the English?... You will never see Grey Lock's name on any agreement with the English dogs! I will abide by the council's decision to keep the peace and lead my warriors back to Missisquoi now. You will find this "treaty" no more valid than the others we have signed over the past two hundred seasons."

"I have no need to speak with Captain Stevens, on this... Tell him however, that if any English come near our sacred Missisquoi, they will have Grey Lock and his warriors to deal with. The Missisquoi tribe will fight to the last man, woman and child to keep our sacred homeland... Go now and sign your agreement. When you return you will find the Missisquoi gone. Peace be with you Metallak, I know you think you're doing the right thing, but I will abstain from this decision. For you my old friend, I give you my plumed long bow. It has guided me through many battles with the white man. Take it now, and may its luck be with you. Adio, old friend." Metallak replies, "Adio, may the spirits travel with you as well."

With that the Missisquoi warriors leave the campsite, climbing into their canoes with their provisions and paddling away upriver in the full moon light. Metallak watches them leave and thinks, "Whether or not you agree with the terms Grey Lock, we've achieved our goal of peace with the English. I could not have done this without you. Adio, Great Chief."

The next morning, Metallak prepares to meet with Captain Stevens to tell him of the Tribal Council's decision. As he does, the sound of many horses riding into Charlestown from the south can be heard. Suddenly, the warriors who were surrounding the town hall come running back towards the fort shouting, "Many more English troops on horseback are coming! Run while you can!"

The sentry in the fort's watchtower shouts down to Captain Stevens, "Sir! We have reinforcements! It appears two companies of the Colonial Militia have just arrived on horseback! What are your orders, sir?" The Captain replies quickly, "To Arms! To Arms! Sound the bugle! All men prepare for battle! Let me see what's going on." Climbing into the watchtower he watches with disbelief as the Militia on horseback are cutting the Abenaki warriors down as they run into the woods.

Stevens thinks, It's the Governor's reinforcements that I requested, but we have not heard the Abenaki's decision on Nathaniel's proposal. I must ride out and stop this now. With that he jumps on his horse and rides out of the fort gate alone holding the Governor's proposal while yelling to the leader of the Militia, "Tell your men to cease fire! We've negotiated a truce. Drop your weapons now!"

The leader of the militia sees Captain Stevens riding out of the fort and orders his troops to hold their fire, but it's too late. The remaining Cowasuck and Sokwaki warriors have taken a position in the woods and are holding off the Militia troops who continue to fire. Many militia troops are shot before they hear the cease-fire orders.

Chief Metallak witnesses this and thinks, Grey Lock was right, never enter into an agreement with the English. Why was I such a fool as to believe them? It is we who are outnumbered now, we'd better fall back and search for an escape route before we're all slaughtered as our ancestors were. He orders his warriors, "Fall back! Fall back! All warriors into the tall pines!" The Abenaki warriors fall back into a grove of White Pines where the Rangers on horseback are unable to follow.

Chapter 17

In all of the commotion Nathaniel rides out of the fort unnoticed. He takes his horse to the far end of the Great Meadow and jumps off by the grove of tall pines, tying his horse to a tree. He sneaks into the Abenaki campsite and finds Chief Metallak unarmed and alone and staring up into a giant White Pine.

He walks up to Metallak and pointing his musket at him he says, "What was the Tribal Council's decision. Did they accept the Governor's proposal? Tell me now!" Metallak replies looking startled, "Nathaniel. I recognize you from the attack at the log sluice. If you have come to slay me, then do so now."

Nathaniel replies, "I haven't come to harm you. I have come to discover what decision the Abenaki Council made on my proposal, which Governor Wentworth granted. Will your people accept the parcel of land for your people to live on without interference in exchange for desisting in your attack?"

Chief Metallak pauses and then points up at the great White Pine saying, "We see two different things when we look up into this sacred pine, you and I. I see a sacred part of the precious land, which my people have left untouched for many generations. You see a large amount of wood, which can be cut down and sliced to pieces to use in building your wooden dwellings, which are scars on the natural Earth themselves."

"As I hear the battle growing nearer and nearer and witness more of my people being killed trying to preserve our beliefs, I realize that your English numbers only grow and grow, as this great tree has, while my people continue to wither and die."

He walks over and points Nathaniel's musket to the ground and says, "My ancestors first met yours when they first arrived on our shores and were fishing in Sobagwa, the great ocean. We welcomed your people to the Dawnlands. You were so few in numbers then and we were many. We never dreamed that your numbers would grow so quickly and ours would become decimated by your muskets and diseases. " Chief Metallak then stares at the ground as a tear comes to his eye, realizing the desperation of the situation.

Chief Metallak looks Nathaniel in the eye while pointing to the Great White Pine and asks, "See this mark scarring the sacred tree? Captain Stevens told me many seasons ago that this mark means that your English King who lives an ocean away "owns" this tree. We Abenaki believe that no man owns any part of the earth and we are privileged to live in the great tree's shadow. Since the Abenaki and all of the native peoples rose from the animals to live in shelters we have always held these beliefs."

"Your English beliefs are very different from ours. In the many seasons since your arrival on our shores, you have scarred the sacred land more than all of our peoples have done in the previous several thousand years combined. If this continues, I can see in the future that all of our forests and trees like this one will become shadows of their former selves, if not destroyed completely."

Nathaniel answers, "Oh Great Chief, I know my people's views on the earth differ greatly from yours. Our peoples hold different views on many things. I am here now to discuss the matter at hand. I have come to find out if you have accepted our offer of peace in exchange for regaining some of your ancestral lands where your people can live unhampered by us and continue their way of life."

"If the tribal council accepted the Governor's proposal, there may be a chance we can end this bloodshed. If you remove your forces to the west side of the Connecticut River, as the Governor requested, then his troops and ours will let your people go in peace to take up your rights in the newly granted land. I discussed this very proposal with Chief Grey Lock before and he seemed favorable towards it. We have little time here, Oh Great Chief, with all due respect what was the councils answer?"

Chief Metallak replies, "The majority of the council accepted your proposal, but Chief Grey Lock would not. He did not believe that this agreement passed the tests of the Sacred Truths and he has left and taken the Missisquoi warriors with him. With all of your new reinforcements, your numbers now equal to or are greater than ours. This has been the continuing pattern of the last few centuries. Your numbers increase while we grow fewer and fewer. Leave my presence now and go continue your battle."

Chief Metallak begins to walk off, but stops when Nathaniel says, "Oh Great Chief, there is still a chance. These troops are under the command of the British Governor. They must follow his orders. If his proclamation states that the Abenaki are to be allowed to move to the granted lands, they must let you do so. Ride out with me under a flag of truce and we will inform the troops of the Abenaki decision."

Chief Metallak turns and replies, "No Nathaniel, as I have already told you, your people's numbers will only continue to grow. As your numbers grow, so will acceptance in your beliefs and way of life. When my people see the advantages of living in warm wooden dwellings and following the progressive English ways, belief in the ancient ways will disappear. Even if we are granted a parcel of land, we will become more and more surrounded by you and eventually the Abenaki will become a forgotten people and refugees in the Dawnlands, our former home."

"Though the Tribal Council voted in favor of your proposal, I now see that Grey Lock was right. The English existence on our shores will only perpetuate your beliefs and annihilate ours. Though today may be the last day of the Abenaki here, remember Grey Lock still lives."

"Behind any tree or hill, he may be waiting to attack and take revenge for this day. You cannot kill him. Grey Lock is more than a man he is the spirit of the Abenaki tribe. The Three Truths will now guide him, as they have my people for all time. Go now Nathaniel; your proposal was a great gesture in a battle that's already been lost. I will lead the final charge myself, and we will go down to the last man for the Abenaki beliefs and the beliefs of all native people."

Chief Metallak walks out of the grove of tall pines and climbs on his horse holding Grey Lock's plumed long bow. He gestures goodbye to Nathaniel as he rides off saying, "Adio Nathaniel, my time has come."

He summons his warriors who are fighting behind the tree line and says, "Sokwaki and Cowasuck warriors, it has been an honor to serve with you all. You have fought with great valor these past days to once again establish our tribe's presence in the Dawnlands. However, the English invaders have received many reinforcements we did not foresee. They now have a force equal to if not larger than our own now. Grey Lock and the Missisquoi have left."

"Though we are outnumbered, we must now make a final charge against the invaders in our last desperate attempt to regain our sacred lands. Though we will most certainly die in this attempt, attempt we must." Chief Metallak pauses and then shouts out, "Are you with me?" The remaining Abenaki warriors let out a fierce battle cry that echoes down the valley.

Nathaniel hears the battle cry as he rides out into the Great Meadow. He sees Captain Stevens conferring with a white wigged man in a stately purple coach surrounded by an entourage of finely uniformed riders just outside the fort's walls. As he rides across the Great Meadow to meet with the Captain, Chief Metallak appears at the edge of the giant pines on his great white horse and raises Grey Lock's plumed long bow signaling the Abenaki attack to begin.

Chief Metallak witnesses Nathaniel about to meet with the Captain and starts charging across the field with another fierce war cry. The Sokwaki and Cowasuck warriors watch their leader charging and storm out of the woods filling the air with loud war whoops.

Startled by the sudden attack, Captain Stevens ushers the purple coach into the fort while raising his silver sword and shouting out, "To Arms! To Arms! Every able bodied man who has a weapon to the Great Meadow now!" All of the men in the fort come out and join the militia troops and outriders in the field opening fire on the advancing warriors. At the same time Ethan Allen and the Green Mountain Boys ride back from the vacated town hall, joining forces with the men at the center of the Great Meadow.

The Abenaki warriors led by Chief Metallak at first appear to have the troops surrounded as they fiercely charge on three sides, but soon they are outnumbered by the combined English forces and are forced to once again fall back behind the tree line.

Chapter 18

While all of the troops are focused on the new Abenaki advance, suddenly the fort gate behind them closes with a loud bang and the sound of Abenaki war whoops begin to come from inside the fort. Captain Stevens hears this and realizes that by bringing all of the men out into the field for the attack, he's left the fort defenseless with all of the women and children inside.

Musket shots and arrows from the fort start reigning down on the Colonial troops as warriors climb to the peak of the Great Chamber's roof and commence firing on the troops in the field. Cannonballs from the fort begin to reign down upon the colonial troops as well, blowing great holes in their ranks and leaving large craters in the earth, while scattering the troops into disarray.

Chief Metallak is surprised by all of this but sees his advantage and orders his warriors to advance back into the field and resume firing upon the confused troops. The Colonial troops are now being fired on from four sides in the wide-open meadow, and suffer many casualties.

Captain Stevens orders his troops to fall back, shouting out, 'Retreat! Retreat!" but there's nowhere to run. As the troops try to fall back into the fort, they are met with more and more fire. As they try to make it to the shelter of the woods, the warriors shooting at them from behind the trees pick them off. The tide of the battle has turned, and Captain Stevens realizes that the Abenaki now hold the advantage.

Stevens looks up into the fort's watchtower and sees the grey visage of Grey Lock standing there staring down at him with a broad grin. He shouts down to the Captain, "Stevens! Your troops are trapped! I now hold your defenseless fort with the women and children trapped inside! You must order your troops to cease fire now, or I will kill everyone inside and throw their lifeless bodies out to you one by one."

He reaches down the watchtower's ladder and pulls up a frightened and trembling Rebecca Jarvis. Calling to Nathaniel while holding a knife to her throat he says, "This woman will die first! What say ye "Nathaniel"? Do you want your wife and child to die? Many more will follow! Ceasefire and surrender now without delay or Grey Lock will have his revenge!"

Nathaniel looks up into the watchtower and sees Rebecca being held by Grey Lock. He calls to the Captain, "Phineas, he has Rebecca! We must come up with a plan before they die. I beg you to order the troops to cease fire!" The Captain acknowledges this and reluctantly shouts out, "All troops cease your fire! Drop your weapons now! There are many innocent lives at stake! All troops drop your arms and raise your hands in the air! This is an order!" Chief Metallak looks on with disbelief as he sees all of the English troops in the field drop their weapons and reach for the sky. He orders his own troops to stop firing and a sudden silence comes over the smoke filled battlefield.

Chief Grey Lock again orders out again over the now silent battlefield, "Bring me the one called "Nathaniel", the English dog who ambushed us in the river and cost many warriors lives. Bring him to the fort gate now or many more will die! Bring all of your muskets to the fort gate as well and pile them on the ground! Do as I say, NOW!" The Captain replies, "It was my plan to ambush you in the river before you reached the fort. Nathaniel was carrying out my orders. Take my life and let the young man live."

Grey Lock answers, "No Stevens, "Nathaniel" will not escape me again. Both of you into the fort at once and kneel at Grey Lock's feet. Stevens, bring me your prize sword as well. I want to have a souvenir of the day the English were made to crawl as you have done to so many of my people over the years. "

The Captain calls out, "All troops do as he says! He has the upper hand on us for the time being. We must protect the townspeople at all costs. Bring all of your weapons and pile them by the fort gate, then return to the center of the field with your arms in the air. That's an order!" Stevens then calls to Nathaniel, "Follow me to the fort gate, we've no choice son."

Captain Stevens and Nathaniel ride to the fort gate and climb off of their horses, tying them to the hitching post. The fort gate opens to allow them to enter as both men drop their muskets and walk inside. The troops begin bringing their muskets to the fort gate and reluctantly pile them on the ground one by one. They return to the center of the Great Meadow standing there defenseless with their arms in the air.

Raising Grey Lock's plumed long bow in the air, Chief Metallak proudly leads his warriors out from the tree line as his warriors advance to close in on the unarmed troops. Grey Lock calls out to him, "Chief Metallak, come inside the fort and join me as we watch the English grovel at our feet. We've much to talk about. Shall we shoot the English dogs one by one or drown them in the river? Our dream is coming true and the Abenaki will rise again!" The Abenaki warriors again begin their war whoops, as Chief Grey Lock still holding Rebecca climbs down from the watchtower and disappears inside the fort while Chief Metallak rides in.

Captain Stevens and Nathaniel walk over to meet Grey Lock as he strides across the fort courtyard. Nathaniel says to Grey Lock, "Well you have us now, release my wife and take us as your prisoners to do with as you will." Chief Grey Lock answers defiantly while releasing Rebecca, "Take the woman. You will die in each other's arms. You and Stevens are now my prisoners "Nathaniel." You will do as I say whether or not I release anyone. You will all pay for your insolence. Many brave warriors died in your ambush and now you will receive your just punishment by *our* laws." He then orders one of his warriors, "Bind them for now, we will deal with them later."

Grey Lock then notices the unguarded purple-cloaked coach at the center of the courtyard inquiring with a devious grin, "And what have we here? Another prize for Grey Lock?" Grey Lock and the warriors closely examine the unguarded coach. They are amazed by the fine cloaks and ornate gold trimmings on the coach and start feeling the unknown fine textures.

He attempts to peer into the coach, but the curtains are drawn. He tries to open the doors but they are latched from inside. Breaking the window glass he unlatches the door and throws it open to find a finely dressed older man wearing an ornate white wig and a very frightened fashionably dressed young woman. He orders his warriors, "Seize them! We have discovered an unexpected prize."

The white wigged man resists the attackers as they try to grab him pointing a pistol at them while he says with rebuke, "Unhand me! I am Royal Governor Benning Wentworth of the Colony of New Hampshire. If you harm my bride Martha or myself in any way I will see to it that you pay dearly. I represent King George the Third, ruler of the British Empire. Desist now I command you!"

The warriors pay no heed to his warnings, they take his pistol from his hand while forcing both he and his young bride out of the carriage. They stand unprotected surrounded by Abenaki warriors at the center of the courtyard, with Martha shaking and clinging to her husband for her very life.

Overhearing Wentworth's words, Chief Metallak rides over to the two saying, "So you are the famous Governor Benning Wentworth of the English Colony of New Hampshire? The one who claims to own all of the sacred trees and Ndakinna from Sobakw, the Great Ocean to Bitawbakw, your Lake Champlain?"

Governor Wentworth quickly answers Chief Metallak, saying authoritatively, "Yes, I am Royal Governor Benning Wentworth of the British Colony of New Hampshire, and whoever lays a hand on my wife or myself will have the whole power of the British Empire to contend with!" Pointing at the men who pulled the two out of the carriage he adds, "You savages are already dead. My outriders will take care of that now. Guards! Guards! Where are my guards?" He shouts, but the outriders are unable to help trapped outside the fort's walls.

Chief Metallak says to the Governor, "Your guards will not help you now, but your name is very familiar to me. For many years now, the English settlers have arrived with their pieces of paper bearing your name, claiming to "own" the sacred land. What power have you over the Dawnlands to claim the land made for everyone as your own?"

Surrounded by warriors, a still commanding Wentworth says, "My authority comes directly from King George the Third, King of England and ruler of the British Empire. I was commissioned by the King in the year of our lord seventeen hundred and forty one to be the Governor of the Province of New Hampshire, as well as the King's Surveyor General. My colony runs from the Northern border of Massachusetts to the southern border of Canada and west from the Province of Maine to the Province of New York."

Chief Grey Lock interjects mockingly, "This man may have power over the English, but he has no power over Grey Lock or my tribes. However, he does have some fine clothes and a woman and carriage that would bring a prime price on the black market." Pointing at Captain Stevens and Nathaniel, being tied to the fort's well he adds, "Bind them with the others for now. We'll deal with them all later."

Suddenly Captain Stevens breaks free from the warriors and

taking his silver sword from its sheath, he comes up behind Grey Lock and puts the sword to his throat saying. "We'll take no more orders from you "Oh Great Chief". Release the Governor now, or I will take your life as surely as you can feel my steel piercing your..." But before can finish another word the whirring of an arrow is heard and it hits Stevens in the arm forcing him to drop his sword.

As the sword clangs to the dirt, Chief Metallak says to Stevens while lowering Grey Lock's freshly fired plumed long bow, "Not today Captain Stevens. My arrow's flight was as true as my people's cause. Today is the day of the Abenaki. You will meet our demands or surely *you* will die."

Grey Lock wipes the blood from his throat onto his hand and offers his bloodied hand to Metallak, who slices his palm with the his knife and shakes Metallak's hand saying. "Thank you my brother. This blood will bind us together as we complete our sacred mission. Now together we will make the English pay for what they have done." Metallak acknowledges as Grey Lock orders his warriors, "Bind the prisoners together, they will all die as one now."

Nathaniel interrupts the Chiefs saying in desperation while pointing at the governor, "Wait Great Chiefs, this man is the Great English Chief who granted your people a homeland of their own. The paper we presented you is a land grant signed by him that will enable the Abenaki to continue to exist with the English in peace. This man has the power to command all of the English in the colony. This man through his authority with the English can grant your people any land you desire."

Nathaniel goes on to say, "Let me tell you as well Great Chiefs, you may have won the battle here today, but if you harm this English Chief in any way, it is true as he says that the English will hunt you to the ends of the earth. Please consider this well as you consider his offer."

Wentworth says to Grey Lock, "Yes, that is true. As Governor, I've granted most of the land in this colony for the last twenty years or so. None of it was exactly for free... But given the situation, I believe I can come to terms with what you savages, err, I mean people want. I will sweeten the pie, so to speak, with more wealth than any of your tribes have ever seen."

Wentworth throws open the rear compartment of his carriage revealing a chest. He unlocks the chest and reaches in to pullout a glittering gold bar saying, "This chest is full of these treasures. This is Spanish Bullion. This is more wealth than all of your combined tribes now possess. I believe there is enough here to buy our freedom. I will trade this gold for our lives and give you the worthless, err, I mean valuable land grant you request as well. Come and see for yourselves."

Grey Lock and Metallak walk to the carriage and look at the chest filled with gold bars in awe. Wentworth hands a bar of the Bullion to Grey Lock and he is surprised by its weight. As he holds it up to the sun both chiefs are fascinated by the way the metal shines.

Wentworth goes on to say to the chiefs, "This metal will give your tribes great wealth and power. More wealth and power than your tribes have ever known. There is enough here to purchase freedom for your people from any invaders for many years. I will give this to you as a token of my people's, uhh friendship. If you set us free, desist in your attack and accept my grant for your lands, all of these gold bars will belong to the Abenaki nation. What say ye to my proposal?"

Grey Lock says defiantly to Governor Wentworth, "As you are our prisoners now, I don't think you'll be making a bargain with us for something we already have. We will take these gold bars from you and leave you and your party lying dead on the ground as you English have done to so many of my people over the years. Warriors take aim!"

"We have not forgotten the Mystic Massacre, or the Pequot tribe." Grey Lock adds, referring to the 1637 massacre of the Pequot tribe, where the English under Captain John Mason surrounded, burned, and killed an entire Pequot village of an estimated 400 to 700 people including women, children, and the elderly who were shot or burned trying to escape the burning walled village.

Wentworth replies, "Yes, I've heard of the massacre it occurred while the Pequot warriors were out on raids in Springfield and I've not forgotten King Phillips War either. Who could forget one in ten of the male English population killed, a dozen of our towns destroyed and our fledgling economy ruined. But that was over a century ago, our people have recovered and yours haven been driven out. I *am* impressed that you have amassed such a force after all of these years. I never would have thought it possible. But let me warn you, if you make a martyr out of my wife and I, King George the Third will hunt you down and destroy all of your so-called people. Your tribe will become as forgotten as the Pequot. Remember this when you consider my more than generous offer."

Chief Metallak calls Chief Grey Lock aside saying, "Let us consider this, Great Chief Wentworth." The two walk a distance away from the carriage and Metallak says to Grey Lock, "This English Chief has great wealth and power, and he is offering our people a valuable prize, we must consider his words. If we accept his offer, our tribes will have the land we so desperately need and enough wealth to repel even the bloody Iroquois to the west to who we pay tribute. His words are true as well that the white man will hunt us down if we kill him on this day. What say ye Grey Lock?"

Grey Lock pauses and then replies staring at the gold bars, "I have seen small pieces of this metal many years ago from the tribes to the west, but never have I seen such a large amount. You are right my brother, these bars will set our tribes free. We hold the advantage now. However, we must act in the best interests of our people and consider the Three Truths before making any decision. What say ye Metallak?"

Metallak answers, "I find that this offer passes all three tests. It will preserve the peace, as we will no longer be warring with the English. It is righteous, as it will complete our sacred mission from the spirits to preserve our way of life. It will preserve our power and integrity by giving us more wealth then we have ever known. What say ye Grey Lock?"

Grey Lock answers, "You are correct on all Three Truths, and I have considered them all as well as you have my brother. I agree to the English Governor's terms. I will sign the treaty."

Metallak answers with a sigh of relief, "Then it's over then. Our sacred mission is completed. I will send word to the tribes and we can now return to our homelands with honor." Metallak then asks Grey Lock, "But why did you return Grey Lock? I'd thought our cause was lost when you left... We were prepared to die in the battlefield. You said you'd never sign a treaty with the "English Dogs." What caused you to change your mind? "

Grey Lock responds, "What is my name?" Metallak replies, "Wawanolet, he who fools others." Grey Lock explains, "Our battle was lost when the English reinforcements arrived. The only way I could see to have a chance at victory was to lead the English to believe that the Missisquoi had left and then sneak back into the fort and use the cannons against them. I knew that the English would be preoccupied with the battle and that I could sneak into the fort with ease, as I've deceived them this way so many times over the many years. I could not tell you of my ruse or there was a chance I would have been found out."

Grey Lock begins to tell his story, "Last night, we paddled our canoes upriver until we were out of sight. We beached the canoes in the full moon light and crept back through the woods until we reached the north side of the fort before daybreak. Then we hid within a short distance of the fort and lay there while the battle raged. With the battle going on the south side, we came into the English fort unseen, seized the fort and used their own cannons against them. With you advancing from the other side they were caught in the crossfire and easily defeated."

Chief Metallak inquires again of Chief Grey Lock, "But still you said you'd never sign a treaty with the English. Why now are you changing your position?" Chief Grey Lock answers, "It took us many moons to build up enough warriors to make this final stand. The English equaled our numbers within a few days. Though my father stood against the English invasion, there comes a time when we have to realize that we're vastly outnumbered and don't have a real chance at victory. The English are here now and the invaders will become the future of these lands. As when man rose above the animals to live in shelters and hunt with the bow and knife, the white man must now lead our species to fulfill their destiny. What we've accomplished here today gives our people another chance at having a homeland. I didn't believe Nathaniel when he told me of his plan, but now I see it is the Abenaki tribe's only chance at survival."

Chief Metallak responds admiringly, "Yes Great Chief, this was your finest tactic in a battle that was won and lost many times. You've earned the right to hold your famous father's name and he would have been proud today of what you have accomplished for our people." Chief Metallak reaches out and shakes Grey Locks hand. Grey Lock answers, "Thank you Great Chief, our people will survive to fight another day. Now let us go give the English Chief our decision."

Both men return to Governor Wentworth's carriage and Chief Grey Lock says to the Governor, "Great Chief Wentworth, we have considered your offer of the yellow metal bars and the land grant in exchange for your freedom and removing our warriors from this side of the great river, and have decided to accept. These bars will give the Abenaki another chance at survival. I will sign the land grant from Captain Stevens now and we will leave on the terms of the treaty to travel to our new homeland. Adio, Great Chief."

Captain Stevens hands the land grant to Grey Lock and he makes his mark. Chief Grey Lock holds the land grant in one hand and addresses his warriors, "Missisquoi warriors, you have performed with honor on this day, and our sacred mission here is completed. We have reached an agreement with the English that will allow our tribes to continue our way of life. Release all prisoners and return to the river. We will now return to our new homeland."

The English troops in the field are shocked as the Missisquoi warriors open the gate and begin to file out of the fort. Chiefs Metallak and Grey Lock lead them out of the fort on horseback and ride across the Great Meadow holding two glittering gold bars and the land grant high in the air for all to see. Chief Metallak calls to the troops, "Retrieve your muskets and return to your homes. We have no more quarrels with your people. Our battle here is ended." The troops pick up their muskets and go about their separate ways.

Chief Metallak instructs his warriors saying, "Oh great Cowasuck and Sokwaki warriors, put down your weapons, our sacred mission here is completed. We have won a new homeland where our peoples can exist in peace with the English. We also have gained enough wealth for our people to become a thriving tribe once again. We must now return to our horses and canoes and leave this place."

With that all of the Abenaki warriors return to the river and the trail north leaving the English troops standing alone in the Great Meadow. Grey Lock rides over to Captain Stevens and says, "Our battle here has ended. You are a formidable opponent and worthy of the honor our people have considered you with for all these years. The Abenaki Chiefs have accepted your terms and I return to you the Fort at Number Four. Adio."

Captain Stevens answers, "I'm glad we could work this out and both our peoples will benefit from this decision. Your father would have been proud of your actions on this day. It has been an honor to face you in battle, and may the spirits ride with you until we meet again. Adio, Great Chief."

Chapter 19

After the Abenaki warriors have left, Governor Wentworth and his wife ride out of the fort in his splendid carriage led by his finely dressed outriders. He recognizes Ethan Allen and tells his coachman to stop the carriage. His wife helps him out of the carriage and he hobbles over and says to Ethan, "Ethan, I didn't expect to see you here... I've had word that the Province of New York has questioned the land grants I sold you. Their claim is based on a vague grant or letters patent made to Prince Charles the Duke of York years ago. Let me ensure you the New Hampshire grants are valid. The Duke of York's letters granted him rights from the Connecticut River to the Delaware, and the King will never validate such a ridiculous claim."

Ethan replies, "I wish the Yorkers believed that. We are fighting every day as more of them lay claims to our granted land and we have to constantly watch our lands for invaders." Wentworth replies, "I've written the King on this and he should be making his ruling shortly. My townships are set up in squares, complete with Christian churches, commons, and modeled after the towns we've already built in the colonies. I've pasted English civilization on the wilderness, so to speak. I believe this pattern will be used as we settle this continent. The New York grants are in oblong shapes with hills and streams for boundaries and no concern for any of this."

"I've also told the Royal Governor of the Province of New York that the Province of New Hampshire will not stand idly by while his settlers move in on already granted lands. It is my hope that King George the Third will set the western boundary of New Hampshire at the Hudson River soon and all the unjust claims will be laid to rest."

Ethan replies earnestly, " We are fighting for our just rights as settlers, and the sooner the King rules on this the better. If His Majesty

doesn't there are many in the Green Mountains who talk of forming
our own independent state."

Wentworth answers, "It will happen Ethan, just give it some time.
Now that this uprising has been settled, I must return to Portsmouth to
attend other duties. Good day sir." Martha helps Wentworth back into his
carriage and the Militia starts to escorts him down the road out of
Charlestown.

Without warning, Ben Jarvis runs out to the carriage and shouts to
Governor Wentworth, "Sir! Sir! So you are the rich Governor who sold my
father his land grant and then told him he couldn't cut the trees on it or he'd
get in big trouble? If a rich King owns the whole world, why does he need
my father's trees?"

Governor Wentworth leans out of the carriage looking down at the
boy and smiles saying, "Yes son. The laws in the Colony of New
Hampshire state that any settler is forbidden to cut any pine tree on his
land over sixteen inches in diameter, and I'll be lowering that soon...
Everyone must pay their taxes to the King and this is just one of them my
boy."

Nathaniel runs to the carriage and says to Wentworth, "Governor
Wentworth, pardon my son sometimes the young ones speak out of place.
Forgive him his insolence, and we will be on our way. It is not the place of
children to be dealing with the laws of government. Please excuse him
Your Excellency, sometimes they know not what they speak of."

Governor Wentworth replies inquiringly, "You're Nathaniel Jarvis
aren't you, the one whose plan has saved the western part of the colony. It
was a brilliant idea to give away land I couldn't sell anyways to stop this
insurrection. You have my gratitude, and the Colony of New Hampshire is
in your debt."

"However, If your son has these rebellious ideas about not

following the King's laws, he must have gotten them somewhere, and usually a child's ideas come from their parents. The King's Broad Arrow Mark is being ignored throughout the colony, and many of the King's Pines are being cut illegally. As His Majesty George the Third needs the White Pines to use as masts for the British Navy, this is not an issue I take lightly."

Nathaniel answers, "With all due respect your Excellency, we colonists are attempting to settle this vast wilderness for the King of England. As his loyal subjects, we must use whatever resources are available to us. The giant White Pines abound in New England and are the most valuable resources available here in this harsh climate. As Governor of the colony, I would think that you would see this and petition the King to allow the colonists to use at least some of the trees. There's a rising tide of Revolution across these colonies and if the King would give in to some of the colonist's demands it may help quell it.

Governor Wentworth opens the door of his carriage and quickly hobbles down to the ground saying, "Your words are treasonous sir, and I could have you shot for even uttering them. I just gave a sizeable portion of the colony to a native tribe, and the colony is still in debt to the Empire for aid we received in fighting the French and Indian War."

"The White Pines have put a sizeable amount of funds in my, err I mean the colony's treasury. Without those funds, I err I mean the colony would be bankrupt. I will not listen to more treasonous talk or ridiculous demands from the common people. The situation here has been resolved and I must attend to more pressing matters of state in Portsmouth. Good Day Sir."

Martha is helping Governor Wentworth back into the carriage when Nathaniel replies, "Ahh yes, Portsmouth. With its cobblestone streets and fine mansions, it's almost like being back in England. As you traveled across the colony on rough dirt roads through the wilderness, it must have been as if you were traveling in another world."

"You must remember Your Excellency where your, "err I mean," the colony's riches have come from. It's from the backs of veterans like myself who fought toe to toe with the French and Indians to win England these lands. All I and many other veterans of the war ever received from our service were these land grants. Parcels of untamed forest in this new world we've settled for the King of England with the sweat of our brows."

"There's a rising tide of Independence here in these colonies. If the King continues to refuse to listen to "ridiculous demands from the common people" he may lose these colonies. No taxation without representation is the modern slogan here. You may want to heed these words for the sake of the Empire."

Governor Wentworth peers out of the carriage window and says with rebuke, "How dare you threaten me! I've a mind to..." Martha intervenes saying, "We do owe this man our lives. Had he not helped stop this rebellion, we would be prisoners now or worse. Will you forgive his insolence for *me*?"

The Governor regains his composure and says, "Well, the colony does owe you a debt Nathaniel Jarvis. In Martha and my gratitude's, you are now allowed to cut any tree on your property without fear of retribution from the crown. Don't utter a word, or I may change my mind. I've heard this talk of Revolution is rising throughout the colonies... I've been governor now for twenty five years, and am preparing to retire. The next governor will have to deal with this Revolution talk."

"Let me remind you sir that the British Empire circles the globe and will not tolerate disobedience of any kind. Our response will be swift and powerful to any type of rebellion. My wife and I will be leaving now, the best of luck to you and all of the colonists on the western frontier. I will leave the militia here temporarily to help with the damages. Good Day. Driver ride on." With that Governor Wentworth's carriage begins its long journey down the winding dirt roads back to Portsmouth.

As the townspeople are making their way out of the fort and back to the village, Nathaniel and Ben find Rebecca and baby Katherine and Nathaniel embraces them. He says to Rebecca giving her a kiss, "This is all over now my dear. We can rebuild our homestead and our new life now. The Abenaki have gone and we can lay your fears to rest." Rebecca replies, "So our dreams are coming true and we will build our shining city in the wilderness as John Winthrop said all those years ago. I'm sorry I ever doubted you Nathaniel. Let's take Ben and Katherine and go home."

Captain Stevens walks over to Nathaniel and shakes his hand saying, "We couldn't have saved this valley without your plan. As preposterous as I originally thought it was, it did work. The whole of the English settlements in the Connecticut River valley are forever in you debt."

Nathaniel replies, "I don't know if this is completely over Captain, but it is a good beginning. The native peoples across America are destined to be downtrodden by the ever-advancing foreign settlers. Our ideals are very different and after speaking with Chief Metallak, I'm not certain whose are the better. When our first settler arrived on these shores we considered them uninhabited except for some wandering savages. Now I see that these people have a civilization that has much wisdom and is much older and possibly better than our own."

"My family and I were forced to leave Massachusetts and come to the Province of New Hampshire in search of a better life because the colony is already becoming crowded and the land is being stripped of its resources at an ever quickening pace. What we have done to this land in the not even two hundred years since we landed at Plymouth is more than the Abenaki and their fellow tribes have done in the preceding several thousand. Who would you say are the savages now Captain, the refined Europeans or the wild native tribes?"

Captain Stevens answers, "That question is not for us to answer Nathaniel and history will decide. What we have done here today at the Fort at Number Four will stand as an example for future generations. Hopefully this will be a new hallmark of these colonies. We've only settled one edge of this continent and I'm sure we've a long way to go to reach the other shore."

Nathaniel replies, "Yes Phineas, I'm sure there are many more cultures that have been established possibly eons ago on this continent that we'll have conflicts with as we settle this land. Our history so far in the New England Indian Wars has been bloody and ended up in the native tribes becoming wiped out. What we've accomplished in Charlestown today could set an example for the next few generations. As we build our shining city on the hill, we should not build it at the expense of the natives."

The Captain answers, "As I said Nathaniel, we will be always in your debt. If you need anything to help rebuild your homestead, we have plenty of supplies in the trading post. Whatever you need feel free to take it free of charge. I'm sure the rest of the settlement will be glad to pitch in and help as well. Feel free to stop in anytime. Good day, sir." The Captain says giving Nathaniel a salute as he walks off.

Josiah Hubbard, Simon Hartwell, and Ebenezer Parker walk by on their way out of the fort and Simon says, " I heard what Captain Stevens offered you from the trading post and the same applies for all of us. Though we're busy with crops and such, if you need help rebuilding your cabin or any stores of food, please let us know. This town will always be in your debt and our doors are always open for you and your family. God bless you, Nathaniel."

Josiah Hubbard grumbles, "Well almost anything, my house was burned down as well and I do need a certain amount of supplies to stay alive." The other men give him a perturbed look and he adds, "Oh well, though my house burned down, I still have substantial holdings around town... Anything for you I guess... My door is open as well." The three men smile and continue out of the fort.

Jacques Pierre and his boys are saddling their horses when Nathaniel walks over and says, "If it hadn't been for your warning Jacques, none of this would have happened and the settlement would have been lost. How can I ever repay you?" Jacques replies, "Your friendship is all I will ever ask of you Mon Ami. Without your solution, all would have been lost. Keep your doors open for my boys and I is all we can ask. Once your cabin is rebuilt, it would be nice to sleep in a real bed instead of the forest floor... and we don't get to taste a woman's cooking very often as well. We must go now and continue on our trader's route. At least my fine pelts weren't lost in all of this. We'll see you again on our way back through and we will take you up on your offer. Au Revoir, Mon Ami." Nathaniel replies, "You can count on it my friend, Au Revoir."

Corporal John Hawkins walks out of Doctor Hastings' house with his chest wrapped in bandages and Nathaniel says to him, "I see those wounds weren't fatal after all." Hawkins answers, "No the Doc patched me up pretty well. Where's Killiam? I should thank him I guess, he did drag me out of there and save my life."

Killiam is standing behind Hawkins, and says, "No thanks needed you grumpy old cuss. Captain Stevens may have done us all a favor by leaving you in the field. We wouldn't have to listen to your constant complaining then." Both men chuckle and walk off towards their lean-to.

Nathaniel stops to reflect as they get on their horses and says to

Rebecca, "Well, Ben and I will have to cut a few more King's Pines now to rebuild our cabin. I hope the Governor doesn't mind... He did give me permission." Rebecca replies not knowing of the Governor's offer, "You know what I've told you about cutting those big pines... She pauses and adds, "Well I guess he wouldn't mind us cutting a few. He does seem like a nice man, and you did save the settlement... Let's go home now and see what is left for supper. I may have some stores in the root cellar the Abenaki didn't find."

Nathaniel replies, "If they did, I can always go shoot that bear that's been bothering you. He does get to be a nuisance..." Rebecca answers scoldingly, "Now don't remind me of the bear. I was thinking all of our troubles are behind us now, and you mention that wild creature. Just when I thought..." But before Rebecca can finish, Nathaniel reaches over and gives her a kiss saying, "Just joking my dear. Now let's go home." The family rides off on the trail north as the sun begins to set in the crimson western New England sky.

As Governor Wentworth and his bride ride down the winding river trail escorted by their Royal Guards, Martha reaches over and gives her husband a big hug, saying in admiration, "When I asked for a little adventure, I never expected that adventure would be an actual battle with muskets blazing... I do not believe I have ever had such an experience in my entire life... You were so brave! I'm so grateful to you Wentworth for bringing me... I do love you. I am a bit famished after our ordeal, however, is there somewhere we can dine in the wild?" Wentworth answers, "I'll have the driver stop at the next Inn we pass. I could use some victuals myself."

As they pass through Walpole an hour or so later they reach the Great Falls, where the Connecticut River drops fifty two feet, and stop to watch the plentiful Atlantic salmon leaping upstream through the river rapids causing the cascading fresh water to sparkle even more in the bright sun. Shouting over the deafening roar of the falls, Martha says to Wentworth, "You were correct Benning, the Connecticut is one of the finest jewels of the colony. It is so wide and has such grandeur. Those leaping fish make it sparkle all the more... and there are so many of them. I can't imagine anywhere in New England where the fishing would be better. Wait, I know those fish. They're the Atlantic Salmon you find so delicious back in Portsmouth. Our servants purchase them for you at the market quite often... though I never had a taste for them. Why are they leaping upriver so far from the ocean? They seem so determined to go upstream."

The Governor answers loudy, "I've been told the salmon make this journey every year to reach their spawning ground at the headwaters of the Connecticut. No one knows why they make this four hundred mile journey simply to lay their eggs. I imagine a saltwater fish must enjoy the fresh water... Perhaps they feel safer laying their eggs in the tall pines where the calm shallow waters keep them away from the dangers of the ocean."

Looking down the tall cliffs to the river fifty feet below they notice seventy five or more circular faces with plumed hair carved into the rocks peering silently down at the ancient fishing spot. Martha says, "The natives here must have chiseled these here for some purpose. I sense a definite pattern, and there are so many of them, covering these cliffs and all facing the same direction... west towards the setting sun. They look so primitive, they are nothing compared to the fine carvings in Europe. They look very, very old though. I imagine the savages in these parts hold some kind of meaning for them."

Wentworth answers, "Yes, these backwards natives are an inferior species and probably never *will* become as cultured as we Europeans. Those primitive carvings *are* no match to the fine art of Europe, as much as their bows and arrows were never a match for our muskets." The Governor pauses and reflects for a moment, "These savages hold a kind of wisdom in their words though, and this place appears to have some sacred meaning for them. Judging by the age of some of these carvings, the natives been coming here for many, many centuries... It *is* too bad their time has come."

Martha looks at Wentworth with a puzzled stare, as he quickly adds, " Ahh Martha, there's your Inn, with a fabulous view of the river at that." He shouts to the driver, "Driver! Stop at that Inn, my lady is famished." Motioning to the Captain of the Guard to halt, the driver answers, "Yes, your Excellency."

The Captain of the Guard then orders the Royal Guard to halt saying, "Dismount. We will be stopping here. Release the horses and tie them to that watering trough for a drink. Find any grain available here in this wilderness to feed them, we've a long journey ahead."

Stopping the carriage in front of the Inn, the driver reaches over and opens the latch on the carriage door. Wentworth hobbles down from the carriage with Martha's help, and leads her up the steps and across the Inn's planked porch opening the heavy oak door.

As the couple enters the Inn, the innkeeper recognizes Wentworth and asks obediently, "Your Highness, how can I be of service today? I feel honored to have the Governor and his beautiful wife dining with us today. We have a fine selection of cuisine here, some directly from the continent. We also have several furnished rooms available if you would like to spend the night. What is your pleasure, your Majesty?"

Wentworth answers, "My good man. My pleasure today is to have some relief from the ordeal my wife and I have been through. I would love some of the fresh salmon, it's always been one of my favorites. Have you any ocean seafood? My wife would prefer bay scallops if they're available." The Innkeeper answers, "Yes, fresh from the coast of Maine. They arrived barely a week ago. It would be my pleasure to serve you and your lovely wife some. Where would you like to sit? Any table for you, your highness." Wentworth answers, "Yes, we would love a seat with a river view to watch the salmon jumping if that's available." The Innkeeper replies, "Yes my lord, only the finest for you. My waiter will escort you to our finest seats with a fine view of the river."

As the waiter leads Wentworth and his bride at the table overlooking the river, Martha asks Wentworth, "What did you mean when you just said their time has come? You have just granted the Abenaki a sizeable portion of land to continue their ways."

Wentworth answers with a smile as he sits down, "I left two companies of militia in Charlestown for a reason. Once back in Portsmouth, I will send them reinforcements with orders to hunt Grey Lock and his kind down and make them pay for what they have done to us. Imagine the thought of the British Empire being brought to its knees by a thousand natives. We've been taming native populations all over the globe for centuries with the spread of the Empire. I gave them that grant because we had no other choice. King George will never approve it as I'm sure he will have reservations about Jarvis's ridiculous plan as well."

He goes on to say, "The British Empire was built on trampling indigenous populations wherever we've gone across the world. These Abenaki and their age old civilization are just another. We are a nation of merchants and shopkeepers. We buy. We sell. But we DO NOT give away... Nothing is free. Once we are back at the Capitol, I will revoke their grant and send another ten companies to the Connecticut to further squash this so called rebellion." He adds with a chuckle, "As I've "given" them the land, I guess we know where they'll be found... Their Chief Grey Lock is known as "the one who fools others"... I've fooled him this day, and may ask for *his* head on a stick to display in front of *my* mansion."

The waiter starts to serve the couple's meal. Martha smells the scallops and says, "And you call these fresh? It turns my stomach with just the smell of them. I cannot eat these, and am now feeling ill. My liege, could we just have some fresh bread for the journey. I'm sure we'll find a better establishment elsewhere."

Wentworth sighs and replies, "Yes my dear, we will take our business elsewhere." He addresses the waiter, "Some fresh bread and crumpets if you have them for our long trip. We will be leaving post haste." The waiter replies handing him two loaves of bread, "Yes your highness, we have no crumpets, but some very fresh bread. Have these two loaves. They will be on the house. I'm so very sorry the meal wasn't up to your standards."

As Martha helps Wentworth out of his chair she glances out the window towards the road to see all of the finely uniformed Royal Guards lying on the ground around the carriage. She says to Wentworth, "Curious... It appears our guards are taking a nap. I guess it's from the stress of the day." A surprised Wentworth replies, "What?" Looking out the window he sees his Royal Guards lying dead in the road with arrows protruding from them.

He calls to Martha as he leaves her and hurriedly hobbles towards the door, "Quickly my dear, we must leave this place!" As he throws open the heavy oak door, he comes face to face with a lone grey faced Indian standing on the porch in silence holding a drawn plumed long bow.